HEART BURN

Also by Anne Cassidy:

ANNE CASSIDY

HEART BURN

TEEN STABBED IN PARK

Police suspect racist motives.

Twenty-two-year-old Joseph Lindsay was stabbed in an unprovoked attack in Woodberry Park on Tuesday night. Unconfirmed reports suggest this was a racist cr... The young m...

was three boys, pinned h wall and kicked hi third assa with a b believ boys

◢ SCHOLASTIC

First published in the UK in 2011 by Scholastic Children's Books
An imprint of Scholastic Ltd
Euston House, 24 Eversholt Street
London, NW1 1DB, UK
Registered office: Westfield Road, Southam, Warwickshire, CV47 0RA
SCHOLASTIC and associated logos are trademarks and/or registered
trademarks of Scholastic Inc.

Text copyright © Anne Cassidy, 2011
The right of Anne Cassidy to be identified as the author of this work
has been asserted by her.

ISBN 978 1407 10779 0

Printed in the UK by CPI Bookmarque, Croydon, Surrey
Papers used by Scholastic Children's Books are made from wood grown in
sustainable forests.

1 3 5 7 9 10 8 6 4 2

www.scholastic.co.uk/zone

ONE

I was waiting for Beth outside Whitechapel tube station when I heard what happened to Tyler Harrington. The news shook me. A whole year had gone by since he and I were together and I was used to people reporting bad things about him. Mostly I just sighed. I'd accepted the fact that he had changed from the lad I once knew. In the last twelve months he had chosen the wrong kind of people to hang around with and had spent time in prison. I knew these things only too well.

Still, the news upset me badly.

The pavement where I was standing was crowded with market stalls doing brisk business. I had to keep stepping aside to let people get by. My best friend, Beth, was late and I kept looking at my mobile to check the time.

The odd thing was that I had been thinking about Tyler since the previous afternoon. I'd seen him while walking home from school. He'd got out of a car about ten metres in front of me. It had taken me only a second to recognize who it was and I'd darted into the doorway of a closed shop to avoid coming face to face with him.

I'd peeked out. He was standing on the pavement speaking on the phone. He had a long coat on over jeans and boots. His hair was cropped and his face was pale. He wasn't wearing his glasses and his free hand was cutting the air as if he was making points while talking. He was looking round but his attention was on the call. His eyes swept across me and I felt this ache in my chest.

He finished the call and put the mobile in his pocket. He walked a couple of steps and then to my dismay he noticed me. He smiled and headed in my direction. I kept my face towards the glass window and studied one of the posters that had been stuck there.

"Ashe!" he'd called.

"Oh, hi!"

"What you up to?" he said, glancing at the poster on the shop window.

I stumbled out some words about looking for a gig to go to. Then I told him about my A levels and Beth and school and my mum and dad and Dan and then I took a breath. I didn't ask him what he was up to because I knew what he did for a living.

"Fancy a coffee?" he said.

"Can't. I've got to be somewhere," I said, stepping out of the shop doorway and making off.

"See you, Ashe," he'd called after me.

I was embarrassed. I had no idea what my hair looked like or if I had a spot on my chin or if he had noticed me earlier watching him from the shop doorway. After about twenty metres I looked round and saw that he was in exactly the same position, staring at me. He raised his hand in a tiny wave and I turned and went on. I didn't look back again.

I'd thought about him on and off during the previous evening. Now, while waiting for Beth, I thought about him again.

I wondered what he was doing. I pictured the funny brown glasses he'd worn to read with and wondered if he still read books by George Orwell. I thought of his room, dark and warm on winter afternoons, and his cat, Sofia, who always seemed jealous of me when I was in there with him. Then I thought of the way we broke up and my throat tightened.

Beth was very late. I pulled my coat tightly round to ward off the cold. Half an hour before I'd left my mum and dad at home amid the debris of unwrapped presents. It was my mum's birthday and I had bought her a pair of art deco earrings and waited patiently for her to open my messily wrapped box. She put them on immediately and I left her looking at them in the hall mirror.

Where *was* my friend? I huffed and watched a small cloud of my breath form. We were due to go to the Victoria and Albert Museum to see an exhibition on twentieth-century fashion. I hadn't really wanted to go but it was important for some of Beth's coursework, and in any case Beth loved the clothes and had been looking forward to it all week. Afterwards we were going to go shopping.

A couple of cars started hooting and there were some raised voices from a group of pedestrians who were ignoring the red man and crossing the road. I looked through the shoppers to see if I could see Beth's cheery face but there was no sign. I took my mobile out of my pocket again and stared at the screen. No text. No voicemail. No call. I wondered what to do. I was stamping my feet with the cold. Something must have happened. Beth wouldn't just leave me standing in the freezing cold for no reason.

Tyler came into my mind again. Today's date was significant. It was a year before at my mum's fiftieth birthday party that I started up with him. For three weeks we'd been together. I'd been this *different* Ashley, a bit wild, reckless even. *What's up with you these days?* my mum had said. *You look different.* Then it stopped suddenly. Like a movie that unexpectedly finished and there was no sequel. It ended badly and left me bruised and even now, a year later, seeing him could turn me to jelly; hiding in a shop doorway, being tongue-tied and unable to speak to him; thinking about him incessantly.

Still no Beth.

I wondered whether to go round her house when I glimpsed a familiar face among the shoppers. A young man in a puffa jacket that was really made for a bigger person. His thin legs stuck out the bottom and ended in big brown boots. He walked towards me with a kind of cocky confidence. Jimmy Connelly, Tyler's mate.

"Hiya, Ashe," he said.

"All right, Jimmy?"

"You waiting for someone?"

"Beth. We're going up town."

He nodded sagely.

"What you up to?" I said.

"Going to the London Hospital," he said, pointing across the road as if I didn't know where the London Hospital was.

"How come?"

"You haven't heard?"

"What?"

"About Tyler?"

I shook my head, trying to look completely unconcerned. A feeling of embarrassment was creeping up my neck, though. It was as if Jimmy Connelly *knew* that I'd been thinking about Tyler. I avoided eye contact and looked over the road, past the cars and lorries and the fog of exhaust fumes to the huge brick building that was the London Hospital. Outside it, there was a giant Christmas tree with lights.

"Tyler got beaten up last night. He ended up in the canal."

"Oh," I said.

"Head injury. Pretty bad, as it goes."

"Is he all right?"

"Three cracked ribs. Cuts and bruises. Broken ankle."

I was shocked. I had expected it to be a black eye, a busted lip, a sprained arm. But cracked ribs, a broken ankle, *a head injury*! This sounded worse than normal.

"He could have died," Jimmy said. "They threw him in the canal."

I pulled my coat tightly round me.

"He clung on to a supermarket trolley wedged against the bank. Otherwise he might have drowned. He said he hung there for over an hour. He said the water was starting to ice up around him."

"How awful."

"They left him for dead."

"Where was it? Do they know who did it?" I said, my mind racing.

"Down by Beckton."

"Was it to do with drugs?"

He shrugged.

A beep came out of my bag. I fished my phone out and saw the word *Beth* on the screen. Her lateness was suddenly explained. Tyler Harrington was Beth's cousin. Her dad and Tyler's dad were brothers. I waited to hear what Jimmy had to say before I looked at the message.

"I thought *you* might be upset," Jimmy said.

"Why?" I said.

"You and Tyler?"

"I'm not upset. I mean I *am* upset. I'd be upset if *anyone* I knew got beaten up."

"Yeah, right."

"Who attacked him?" The name *Billy Rob* came into my head but I didn't say it.

"No one knows. No witnesses. It was one o'clock in the morning. Tyler's not saying anything."

"It's not *life threatening*, though?"

"Not as far as I know."

"But you've seen him?"

"In A and E. He called me about three this morning. I went straight up there. I left when they took him to the wards. He looks a mess but he was talking."

I still had my mobile in my hand. I couldn't think of a word to say. He'd been on my mind since the previous afternoon and now this. It seemed uncanny. Yesterday I'd seen him up and fit. He'd looked good, too good. It had thrown me into a reverie. I had almost been *enjoying* thinking back over those weeks.

Now this.

I looked down at my mobile and pressed the button to read Beth's message.

Some probs here. My cousin's been hurt. Have to look after Sara. Beth.

"Better go," Jimmy said. "Shall I give Tyler your love?"

"No!" I said, indignant.

Jimmy walked off through the milling shoppers, his big boots moving surprisingly swiftly. When he had crossed the road and disappeared into the front of the hospital, I had a moment's indecision. The entrance to the London Hospital was thirty or forty paces away. Apart from the previous afternoon I hadn't spoken to Tyler for a long while. I'd seen him around. He was often in pubs, at gigs or parties, selling a bit of dope or stronger stuff. I'd seen him with a black girl a couple of times and wondered if she was his girlfriend. Beth had told me that he'd moved out of his mum and dad's house and shared a flat with Jimmy Connelly and some other lads.

Would it be a good thing to visit him?

I took a step towards the crossing that led to the hospital, but then I stopped. What would I say to him? Why on earth would he want to see me? Stupid, *stupid*.

I walked away, through the market, leaving the London Hospital behind me. I made myself think of other things: Beth, the exams, my coursework, my mum's birthday, my brother Dan, who was due home next week from university for his Christmas break. After a few minutes, though, my mind went back to Tyler. I pictured him in the filthy freezing water, holding on to a supermarket trolley, his fingers laced through the wire mesh, shouting out so that someone would hear him

He'd needed help and there had been no one to give it to him.

It gave me this *crushing* feeling in my chest.

I pushed it down and headed for home.

TWO

I shoved my hands in my pockets and walked briskly. In one pocket I felt my purse and my travel card; in the other was my bunch of keys. I fiddled with my key fobs and tried to recapture the good mood I had had that morning.

Christmas was everywhere. As I passed the shops I could hear the singles that were played year after year. The decorations and the glitter seemed at odds with the grey streets, and every shop appeared to have a container of wrapping paper outside with a sign that said *Three for two*. There were still twenty-one days to go and yet Christmas seemed like it was round the corner.

It made me think of the present I had bought for Tyler a year before. It was a 1960s West Ham football shirt. It was claret and blue and I'd got it down the market. I'd bartered for it and got a couple of quid off, which meant it was most certainly a fake, but that hadn't mattered to me. I'd wrapped it up in Christmas paper, making the usual mess of the corners. I'd even stuck some little heart-shaped stickers on it. Tyler and I broke up before I could give it to him.

I opened my front door and went into a rush of heat. It was welcome. My nose was wet at the end and the tips of my ears felt grated by the cold air. I leaned against the radiator as I peeled off my gloves and my coat. My mum was just coming down the stairs. She was still wearing the earrings I'd bought her.

"Great earrings," I said.

"My absolute favourite birthday present, but don't tell Dad," she said. "You're back early. Thought you were off to the V and A?"

"Long story."

"You haven't fallen out with Beth?"

I shook my head. "Beth's cousin has been beaten up. He's in hospital. . ."

"That lad you were keen on?"

"I hung around with him for a while. It was no big deal. . ."

"*Taylor* something."

"Tyler Harrington. Same surname as Beth," I said, a little testily.

"You did like him. For a while as I remember. . ."

"It was just one of those things," I said, turning sideways so that I could get past her up to my room.

I opened my laptop and turned it on. I shuffled my papers around and tried to get down to some work. I had to distract myself. I had to get Tyler off my mind. I had coursework that was due in before Christmas and I'd already made a first draft. I waited for the computer to load up and watched my fingers tapping intently on the desk surface. I tried to relax. I looked for the right file and double-clicked, trying to keep myself busy. The document opened and I read over what I'd already written. Then I had a burst of energy and added a few more paragraphs. I paused for a second, pleased that I'd used all my frustrations with the day to get on with my work, when the screen went blue.

I sat looking at it with disbelief.

"Mum!" I called out. "My laptop's crashed again! That's twice this week!"

There was no answer from downstairs. My mum had had enough of me moaning about my laptop, about how old it was and how I needed a new one. I pressed a few more buttons but the screen stayed the same: blue with words and symbols on it. It might as well have had a picture of an explosion blowing my work to smithereens. I snapped the lid shut in a temper and went downstairs to make something to eat.

Beth came after lunch. She was grumpy, but as usual she was perfectly groomed. She had polka-dot leggings on and a white fitted fifties-style sweater. Over the top was a Burberry mac that she had found in a charity shop some weeks before and hadn't stopped wearing. Beth looked like a fashion model.

She made a face as she came upstairs to my room.

"I heard about Tyler," I said. "I saw Jimmy Connelly down by the tube."

Beth shrugged. "Sorry about leaving you standing."

Her eyes went glassy. I could see she was on the brink of tears.

"Are you worried about Tyler?" I said.

"It's always the same!" she said passionately. "Whenever anything happens I'm left babysitting."

"But if Tyler is badly hurt, you can understand. . ."

"Mum knew I had something special to do today!"

"If Tyler's in hospital, though. She is his aunt."

She sighed. She pulled out a small white handkerchief. Beth was the only person I knew who didn't use tissues. She dabbed her eyes with it.

"Mum said Tyler might have pneumonia."

"Pneumonia?" I said, alarmed.

"He was in the freezing canal."

"Jimmy Connelly didn't say that. Perhaps he didn't know. . ."

"It was only a matter of time. That's what my dad said. You know since Tyler got out of prison he's been hanging round with some bad types. . ."

"He might have *died*," I said.

"Well, he's having an operation this afternoon."

"An operation? For the head injury?"

There was a sound from downstairs.

"They have to fix the bones in his ankle. . ."

It was the front door opening. My mum's voice rang out with squeals of delight. Then I heard my brother's gruff tones.

"Dan's back?" Beth said, brightening up. "Have they broken up at uni?"

"I don't think so," I said, walking out on to the landing, puzzled.

"Hi, sis! Hi, Beth," Dan called up the stairs.

We both called back down to him. My mum was fussing round, acting as though she hadn't seen him for months when it had only been a few weeks. She pulled him by the hand towards the kitchen and I focused on the giant rucksack and two heavy-looking bags that sat on the floor of the hall. It looked as though he was planning a longish break.

"You didn't tell me your brother was coming home," Beth said, putting on some Chapstick.

"I didn't know."

"Maybe he's come home to see a girl?"

"Dan hasn't got a girlfriend. I told you."

Beth looked into my mirror and fluffed her hair up.

"How about a quickie trip to Wanstead?" she said.

I nodded. Why not? Wanstead was five stops on the Central Line and there were six charity shops. It was better than nothing.

I got back about five. I had two bags full of things I'd bought. I'd found a pair of Levi jeans and a Fair Isle jumper with a reindeer on it which I thought would be funny and look retro on Christmas Day. In the other bag was a dress which I didn't like much but which had been made from pretty cotton fabric, so I thought, with the help of my mum, I might be able to make it into something else, a top or a skirt for the summer. In all I'd spent about six quid.

Beth had been on good form, trying to persuade me to buy a shoulder bag that looked quite smart. But I didn't like bags. I preferred to have pockets in my clothes. All I needed to carry was my purse, my travel card and my keys. I couldn't be bothered with a bag hanging off my shoulder.

Dan's bags had been moved from the hallway and I could hear music coming from his room upstairs. I went into the kitchen and saw Mum sitting glumly at the table. Before she spoke I knew what she was going to say.

"Dan's not going back to university."

I sat down, my carrier bags dropping on the floor beside me.

"Maybe he just needs a break."

She shook her head. It was something unusual when Mum had nothing to say.

"I'll make some tea," I said, getting up, giving Mum's shoulder a stroke as I passed.

The fact that Dan wasn't going back to university wasn't a surprise. Dan had been at university for three months and hadn't taken to it. I'd received emails from him every few days moaning about the place, the other students and the lecturers. At least a couple of nights a week I'd heard either Mum or Dad on the phone to him persuading him to stay, to give it some time, to look for the positive, not the negative.

"What he's going to do?" my mum said, exasperated. "It's not like he can get a job! He'd never settle. He's not like you!"

I knew what she meant. Dan was Dan, always changing his mind about stuff. When he was in year ten he wanted to work with animals and my mum got him information about becoming a veterinary nurse. In year eleven he wanted to have his own band and Mum bought him a keyboard. In year twelve he wanted to be a DJ and Dad bought him turntables. By the time he was applying for university he wanted to be a music producer, so my mum found out about a music-related IT course. Every few months he seemed to change his mind. He was two years older than me but seemed so much younger. I had always been the more sensible of the two of us. He knew it and I knew it. It didn't seem to cause any trouble between us. I was his *big* sister and I didn't mind it one bit.

The sound of singing came from the hallway. It was my dad coming down the stairs.

"Dad's not upset, then."

"Dad says to leave him to sort it out himself, but I don't like to. I worry about him. . ."

I did understand. Dan had had some troublesome years and my mum hadn't known the half of it. I knew that she was worried in case he wasted the chance he had at university. I secretly thought that Dad's plan might have been a better one. Leave Dan to sort himself out.

But Mum couldn't.

My dad appeared. He gave me a distracted smile and then went off into the living room. It only took a second for the TV to come on with the sound of a football commentary. Mum rolled her eyes at me.

After I made Mum a cup of tea I walked upstairs to my room. I upended my plastic bags and shook out my purchases. I was really pleased with the jeans. Beth had looked at them jealously, but they'd been my size, not hers. I opened my wardrobe and put them on a hanger. The dress I folded up for later. I went on tiptoes and put it on the high shelf. My fingers snagged on a plastic bag which I edge towards me. I pulled it down. Through the plastic I could see the claret and blue of the West Ham shirt that I'd bought a year before to give to Tyler as a present. I wondered what was happening at the hospital. Was he under anaesthetic? Being operated on? More to the point, what kind of bad trouble had Tyler got himself into?

I had a gnawing feeling of unease. Did it have anything to do with Billy Rob and the stuff that happened last Christmas?

I shrugged my shoulders. It was nothing to do with me.

Tyler had made his choice a year ago.

THREE

I was coming out of school on Monday afternoon with Beth when I saw a car pulling up on the zigzag lines outside the gate. The passenger door opened and Jimmy Connelly got out. He stood for a second speaking to whoever was inside the car, then he patted it on the roof and watched as it drove off. I wondered what he was doing there.

"Has Dan decided whether or not he's going back to uni?" Beth said.

We were walking towards her bus stop.

"He says he's definitely not going back," I said.

"So he'll be living at home?"

I nodded. I had been waiting for Beth to ask me a direct question about Dan all day. There had been one or two hints.

"Everything all right at home?"

"What did you do last night?"

These had been questions designed to get me talking about my brother. Now at least she was being straight. Not that I had been any better. I was eager to know about Tyler's condition. The previous day Beth told me that the doctors had operated on his ankle to reset the bone and titanium pins had been put in place to hold the joint. They'd kept him in hospital because his temperature had gone up. He was feverish and they were worried about infection. The word *pneumonia* kept coming into my head.

I'd been keen to ask her about him all day but felt awkward.

"We'll have to go out somewhere. The three of us," Beth said.

As we got nearer to her bus stop I looked round and saw Jimmy walking about twenty metres behind us. When I turned again a few moments later I saw that he wasn't exactly *walking*, he was ambling along as if he were out on a stroll.

"How's Tyler?" I said.

"I haven't heard anything new."

"Right," I said, looking round and seeing that Jimmy had stopped at a furniture shop and was looking in the window.

"You seem very concerned about Tyler. I thought you said that it hadn't been serious between you two?"

"It wasn't."

"Like, you haven't mentioned his name all year and now suddenly you're asking about him every day."

"Because he got hurt. That's all!"

"Um. . ."

"Here's your bus," I said.

"See you tomorrow? Meet here?"

I nodded. Beth and I always met at her bus stop and walked the short distance to school from there. Sometimes we stopped and had a hot drink at Chaplin's Café. Sometimes we went straight to school and had something from the machine in the sixth-form common room. We always needed a drink and chat every morning before lessons started.

Beth edged forward with the rest of the students and got on the bus. I watched it pull away. I thought about Beth saying that *it hadn't been serious between you two*. It reminded me that during the few weeks that Tyler and I had been together Beth's pregnant mum had been taken into hospital because of high blood pressure. There'd been a chance that she might lose the baby and Beth and her dad had been up and down the hospital every day. It meant she'd hardly been around those few weeks. When her mum came out of hospital with Sara she had been needed at home. She'd had to take time off school and missed some of her mock exams and then I hardly saw her all over Christmas. She'd been miserable as hell, but the baby had made up for it a bit, and by the time her mum got back on her feet my *thing* with Tyler was history and all Beth had known was that we'd spent a bit of time together. *I don't know how you could stand him, he's such a loser,* she'd said.

I turned away from the bus stop and saw Jimmy on the other side of the road. Was he following me? I walked to the next corner and then stopped. He was still there. Exasperated, I stared at him. He looked sheepish and came across the road.

"What are you doing?" I said.

"Hi, Ashe," he said as though he'd only just noticed me. "How's school?"

"*Sixth form* is OK."

"Doing exams?"

"Some, in January."

"I don't know how you stand it. Books, books. Writing essays. Drove me mad."

"Really? I had no idea you were ever at school, Jimmy."

"Very funny."

"Why are you following me?"

"Tyler wants to see you. He asked me to *ask* you to go and see him."

"Why?" I said.

"Maybe it's *lurve*," he said, adopting a funny face.

"Don't . . . be stupid," I stuttered. "I've hardly spoken to him in the last six months."

"Still he asked me to ask you to come and see him tomorrow afternoon at two. Victoria Ward. There won't be anyone else there."

I shook my head.

"He *really* wants to see you."

I had an odd feeling; a flicker of heat in my chest. It took me back a year. During those weeks that I was with Tyler I seemed to spend most of my time rushing back and forth to his house. His parents were at work and I had study leave for my mocks. My jacket always seemed to be flapping open, my school bag hanging off one shoulder. I was half walking, half running round the streets to get to his house so that we could spend time on our own. The weather was bitter, it even snowed, but I was always hot, my cheeks flushed, my skin searing.

"What shall I tell him?"

Jimmy was looking at me intently. I turned away. The traffic was at a standstill and it reminded me of a time some months before, in the autumn, when I was standing waiting to cross the road. The cars were queuing and my gaze settled on a silver car that was idling close by me. Tyler was in the passenger seat. He didn't see me; he didn't even look out of the window. He was in deep conversation with a black girl who was driving. Her face lit up with a smile as he talked and then she put one of her hands out and mussed his hair. I had felt this hot jagging pull in my chest and turned away, walking further along to cross between two other cars.

I'd seen them again a few weeks later outside a pub we went to. They'd been talking quietly. He'd had his face close up to her ear and it had made me wince and back away, afraid that he would see me watching him. I'd ducked into the pub and edged through the crowd to the Ladies' and looked at myself in the mirror, my eyes glinting with tears.

"Well?" Jimmy said.

"I can't. I'm sorry."

I walked off, determinedly gathering speed so that Jimmy wouldn't follow. When I got home I could hear music from upstairs. Dan was playing his keyboard, a sound I hadn't heard for a while. I went up to my room and threw my bag and coat on the bed. He sounded like he was in full creative mode so I decided not to bother him. I opened up my laptop and turned it on. I was determined to do some research for an assignment in art history. I went on a few websites and cut and pasted material that I thought I might use and saved it in a file. I did it methodically, efficiently avoiding the usual temptations of sliding off on to Facebook and dithering among the pages.

How odd! Tyler asking me to go and see him.

I stopped what I was doing for a second and pictured him the previous Friday standing on the street, his long coat making him look smart and grown up. I imagined myself putting my hand out and touching the collar, running my finger down his sleeve. I saw myself taking his hand and pulling him into the empty shop doorway.

"Ashe!"

My brother's voice sounded. I opened my eyes and saw that the screen of my laptop had gone blue. I swore at it in frustration. I heard Dan call me again and I got up and walked across the landing to his room.

"Hi," he said. "Listen to this."

He played a short piece and I shrugged.

"Don't be too overwhelmed," he said.

"I'm in a mood! My computer's gone down again. I keep losing so much stuff!"

"Buy a new one?"

"With what?"

"Use a memory stick?"

"I keep losing them. They're so small, they get stuck in

a corner of my bag or skid across the desk and fall on the floor."

He turned back to the keyboard and started writing on a pad.

"Still not going back to uni?" I said.

He shook his head. "No way."

He'd already told me all about it. The course was not what he'd thought it would be. There was too much theory and not enough hands-on computer or music work. The other kids were beginners, whereas he'd been working with music since he was a kid. Most of the students there wanted to party morning, noon and night, and the halls were filthy. The shared kitchen was so bad that his feet stuck to the floor when he went in there. He'd hated it.

"What are you going to do with yourself?"

"I'll work something out."

"Has Mum tried to change your mind about it?"

"Not yet."

There was quiet for a few moments. He turned back to his keyboard and played some notes.

"Remember Tyler Harrington?" I said. "He got beat up on Friday night. Badly hurt. They threw him in the canal."

Dan stopped playing again. "I know. Mum told me. He hangs around with some bad people, Ashe."

"Yeah," I said, the words coming out before I could stop them, "that's why everyone was able to buy drugs from him."

Dan stared at me for a moment, a hurt look on his face.

I shouldn't have said it but I couldn't help myself. I looked down at the duvet cover.

"There were loads of people who sold drugs. You don't know the half of it," he said.

It was on the tip of my tongue to tell him that I did know, but what was the point?

"Is he going to be all right?"

"I expect so," I said, in a flat voice.

"You never did quite get over him, did you?"

"I *did*," I said. "It was only a few weeks' thing. . ."

"Yeah, if you say so."

Later, in my room, I looked at my diary and saw what work had to be ready for the next day. After sorting out my papers I sat down on the bed, deflated. The ongoing news about Tyler was affecting me. The request from Jimmy that I visit him had thrown me completely. It did seem, in the last couple of days, as though I had gone back in time and feelings were spilling out that had been tightly packed away for a whole year. During that year I *had* been affected by news of Tyler. When he was sent to prison I was upset but I'd kept it to myself. When I saw him around selling dope or at parties or in pubs I usually made myself scarce. Even when I saw him with the new girl I buried the hurt. I never spoke to anyone about him. Most of the time I was fine. I was over him, I was past it, I was moving on. And yet apart from a kiss and a cuddle with a couple of lads in the sixth form, there hadn't been anyone else for me the whole year. I just hadn't been interested.

I looked at the diary. Then I opened my desk drawer

and riffled around, pulling out last year's diary. I turned to the pages of a year before.

On Saturday 4th December I had written *Mum's Fiftieth Party!!!!* It had been held in a room above a pub. Mum and Dad encouraged me and Dan to invite friends: *As many as you like!* It was embarrassing, though. A room full of aunts and uncles and Mum and Dad's work friends. Dan brought a few mates. I only brought Beth.

In my diary, I had drawn a tiny heart on this date.

It was the first night that I got together with Tyler Harrington.

The pub was called The Cheese and Ale. My mum and dad chose it because it had an upstairs room that was just big enough for a family "do". It had a long food table which had been decorated with flowers and helium balloons and in the middle was a big cake in the shape of the number 50. Around the room were streamers and packets of party poppers. It had been nice to see some of the relatives, but it wasn't the sort of party that I liked to go to. There was a disc jockey who kept playing tunes that made me and Beth roll our eyes. He kept saying, *Now here's one for the young uns. . .*

Dan was grumpy. He'd had a row with Mum before leaving the house. I'd tried to make peace and he'd told me to mind my own business, so I was mildly huffy with him. He'd been a bit off for weeks. His turntables sat in the garage unused and he had started hanging round with a number of odd-looking lads and girls who he'd hooked up with at a music festival. I'd see them with him in The Drake, a pub we all used that had a back room for bands. His new friends hadn't come to the party and he was sitting with three kids I recognized from the sixth form. One by one they kept disappearing off to smoke.

"I wonder what they're smoking?" Beth said.

"I wonder," I answered.

Dan was allowed to drink alcohol and most of his friends had beers in front of them. Beth and I were not allowed to drink so we stood around with glasses of lemonade. Every now and then we went downstairs into the Ladies' and Beth fished out the half bottle of vodka she'd brought in her handbag and tipped it into our glasses. Then we skipped back upstairs to the sound of the DJ singing along with one of the songs.

I spent a long time smiling at relatives and declining to dance with my dad. I was thoroughly bored, so when I noticed Dan getting up to go downstairs I gave Beth a nudge.

"Let's catch Dan smoking dope," I said.

We followed him down through the bar and stood at the door as he went into another room where there was a row of machines with games and quizzes on them. A couple of people were playing at them. One of them was Tyler. I recognized him from the days when he did still go to school.

"There's your cousin," I said to Beth.

She made a disparaging sound.

My brother standing talking to him. That didn't surprise

26

me because they had both been in the same year at school. After a few moments Tyler turned and walked out of the bar via the door that led to the Gents'. Then Dan followed him.

"Do you want a refill?" Beth said.

I shook my head. I was curious as to what my brother was doing with Tyler. They were so different. There was no way they ever hung around together at school. Dan was a music nerd and Tyler was involved in sports and bunking off. They were mismatched. They looked awkward together; Tyler was taller and broader, wearing a dark jacket over a football shirt and jeans. My brother was smaller and thinner. He wore baggy jeans and had at least two T-shirts on, one over the other. Around his neck was a set of beads.

"Wait here," I said, and walked through the bar towards the door which they had left by.

A cold hallway wound past the Ladies' and the Gents' towards an outside door and a sign that said *Smoking Area*. I didn't go out; I just looked through the glass section of the door. There were several people sitting underneath a wooden canopy, huddled in their coats smoking, some with drinks in their hands. The roofing had lantern-style lights and they were swaying in the wind. The smokers looked very cold. Dan and Tyler were not smoking. Dan was talking animatedly to a man who looked like he might have come from a wedding reception. He had a grey suit on with an open-necked shirt. He didn't look cold. He could have been a businessman on his way home from work but he looked too young. Behind him were the lights of a car and I got the impression it was waiting for him. I stayed for a while longer but it didn't look as though Dan was going to take out a roll-up and smoke it.

"Come on!" a voice said.

Beth was behind me. I turned and followed her back into the pub and we went back upstairs to the party.

"How come you didn't say hi to your cousin?" I said.

"We don't speak to him. He upset my mum a few weeks ago."

"Oh."

Dan came back into the party then and rejoined his mates. He had cheered up and beckoned for us to go over to their table so we did. Beth nodded enthusiastically at every word he said. I was bored. My glass was empty and I was gasping for a beer. I decided to go downstairs and buy one. I knew I could pass for eighteen. I'd done it before.

As I was paying for the beer I felt a hand on my arm.

"Hi, Ashley. Let me pay for that."

It was Tyler. He had a twenty-pound note in his hand. The barman took it and turned away to the cash register.

"Thanks," I said.

"Where's Beth?"

"Upstairs. It's my mum's fiftieth birthday party."

He nodded.

"My cousin doesn't speak to me," he said.

I noticed a pair of glasses sticking out of the pocket of his jacket.

"My own family don't speak to me most of the time," he said, shrugging.

"What have you done?"

"Just being myself. It seems to upset people. I don't know why. Do I upset you?"

I smiled and shook my head. An odd feeling was coming over me. It was part embarrassment and part something else. I was suddenly tongue-tied.

"What?" he eventually said.

"I didn't know you wore glasses."

I cringed. How could I say something so banal. *Stupid, stupid.*

"Ah," he said, taking them out and putting them on, "I need them to read my book."

The glasses transformed him. They had light brown speckled frames and made him look serious.

"What you reading?" I said.

He pulled a book out of an inside pocket of his jacket. It was a paperback with curled corners. I looked at the cover. *Animal Farm*, George Orwell.

"I read that," I said. "Didn't like it."

He put the book back and took his glasses off. I wanted to say something really interesting about books or the pub or his football team but my mind went blank.

"I ought to be going back to the party. Thanks for the drink."

"Come and sit down. They won't miss you for five minutes," he said, staring at me, making me fidget with my beer. "I'll persuade you that *Animal Farm* is a good book."

I looked at the doorway to the upstairs of the pub. I had a choice. Rejoin the party or stay downstairs and talk to Tyler Harrington. I thought about it for two seconds; then I followed him to a table.

The next day I opened my diary at the page for 4th December and under the words *Mum's Fiftieth Party!!!* I drew a heart.

Now, a year later, I looked at it again. It was a heart that could have been sketched by a five-year-old. I couldn't help but smile. My pleasure was mixed, though, tinged with bitterness for what came after.

FOUR

I was at the bus stop waiting for Beth when I noticed Jimmy in the distance. He was walking in a determined way. There was none of the silly playing around of the previous afternoon. He was heading for me, I could tell.

There was no sign of Beth's bus.

It was a windy day and my hair was all over the place. I held it down with one hand, moving from side to side when the wind changed.

"Hi, Ashe."

"Hi, Jimmy."

He came straight to the point. "I told Tyler what you said."

I ignored his tone and peered round his shoulder, thinking that I could see a bus in the distance.

"How is he feeling?"

"Not so good. He's in a lot of pain."

He seemed to be fiddling with something in his pocket. The bus was coming closer and so I could make out the number. It was Beth's bus. I was glad of that because it would mean I wasn't on my own with Jimmy.

"I'm waiting for Beth," I explained.

The bus was stopping and I could see Beth standing

behind the doors. I could feel Jimmy staring at me. Why wouldn't he go away?

"Tyler asked me to give you this."

I looked round. He was holding out a pink envelope that had been folded in half. He gestured at me to take it. I did and he promptly walked away. Without a word. I felt the envelope and then read the name written on the front. In was in my handwriting. *Tyler*. Beside it was a drawing of a heart. All my own work. How many hearts had I drawn during those few weeks?

Beth was beside me.

"What's that?" she said.

"Nothing," I said, shoving the letter in my pocket.

We walked on to school with Beth talking about her coursework and her mum and how Sara had been in her room again even though she had expressly forbidden it. I was only half listening. I felt a cloud hovering above me. This contact with Tyler was getting me down. I felt like telling Beth but she had been in the dark about my feelings for her cousin. It had suited me at the time because I knew that Tyler wasn't ideal material for a boyfriend. I think I knew from the word go that I would come out of it a bit bruised and maybe for that reason I deliberately hadn't wanted Beth to know how I felt. In any case he was her *cousin*. I didn't want her feeling awkward.

Once we got to the common room I went into the loo. When I came out Beth was talking to some kids we knew so I went and sat on one of the soft chairs. After a while the bell for registration went and people started to move off.

"You coming?" Beth said.

"I'll be along in a minute. Just got something quick to read."

I sat looking out of the common-room window at the latecomers running through the gates. I could feel the letter in my pocket. I could sense it there, just coloured paper and handwriting. I was tempted to take it out and read it over but something stopped me. I stared at the school gates and remembered the time, a year before, on the Tuesday after my mum's party, when I walked out and saw Tyler standing across the street. He'd grinned at me and I'd blushed, aware of my navy skirt, black shoes, my striped tie and my rucksack full of school stuff. I felt about twelve years old.

"Hi."

I'd glanced past him as if he wasn't anyone special. My shoulders were rounded, and I walked on, forcing him to quicken his pace to keep up with me.

"Slow down," he said.

I stopped. "What are you doing here?"

"Desperate to see you!"

I tried to keep a straight face. I tried to be cool and detached, to show I wasn't much affected by Saturday night. I wanted to make it clear that being kissed by a bad boy like Tyler meant nothing to me.

"I've been pining for you all day!"

He had both hands over his ribs where his heart was. I

smiled. I couldn't help it. Inside I was like jelly. The idea that *he* was desperate to see me when I had been thinking him about ever since.

"My mum and dad are out for the night. My house is empty. Why don't you come round?" he said.

"What for?" I said.

"To spend some time on our own?" he said.

I immediately frowned. On Saturday night, when we'd been out in the smokers' area at the back of The Cheese and Ale, I had been dizzy with the kissing but suddenly alert when I felt his fingers undoing the buttons on my top. I'd pushed him away and he'd laughed at me. Being alone with him, in his house, I might find it more difficult to hold back. I began to shake my head.

"But I ought to say up front," he said, "there'll be no kissing and stuff. I've got my reputation to think of."

I didn't know whether to frown or laugh. I tried to think of some pithy answer but my mind was a blank sheet.

"Will you come?" he said.

We stood on the pavement as numbers of school students walked in between us and around us. He was waiting for an answer and I was looking down at my shoes: black leather, sensible design, low heel, square toe.

"I've got to revise for my mocks."

"Come back to mine," he said, "I'll show you my revision notes from last year."

"Your notes? You were never in school!"

"Come back," he said, "you can show me what I missed."

I looked at him. His eyes held me to the spot.

"Come. . ." he said, his hand out to take mine, his voice in a whisper.

I went to his house that day. And the day after. And over the next couple of weeks I went to his house whenever I had study leave. Instead of revising for my GCSEs I spent time with him.

I learned a lot over those days, and some of it was still hurting me.

The sixth-form common room was empty. There was a hush that I had never noticed before. The school gates had closed over and everyone was in their form class. They'd be sitting listening to the announcements for the day, being told which lessons had substitute teachers and which groups had to move to another room because of timetabling changes. There might even be a little pep talk or a five-minute targets session.

I put my hand in my pocket and felt the pink envelope. I took it out and unfolded it. I slid the letter out. I hadn't written much.

Tyler, you are brilliant! I owe you xxxxxxxx

Underneath, in shaky writing, with a pencil, he had added the words *You owe me X.*

I wasn't sure what affected me the most. Him pressuring me to go and see him or the kiss he had written. Either way I knew then that I would go and visit him in Victoria Ward that afternoon.

FIVE

The hospital was full of signs in different languages and it took a while for me to find the one for Victoria Ward. I headed off for the lift and joined a crowd of people carrying bunches of flowers and a helium balloon that said, *It's A Boy!* They were chatting excitedly, their faces split with smiles. The ward was on the second floor and I left the happy family in the lift and headed towards it. I shoved my hands in my pockets. I grabbed my bunch of keys and felt the various fobs digging into my skin. I had a jittery feeling in my stomach.

The door to Victoria Ward was open and some people were walking in ahead of me. I was dearly hoping that I wouldn't run into Beth's mum and her sister-in-law but Jimmy had said that I would be the only visitor. I paused behind a couple of people in front to run my hands under the alcohol hand rub. Then I walked up to the nurses' station. Three nurses had their heads bent over computers and I waited for a few seconds.

"Excuse me, I'm looking for Tyler Harrington?" I said in a polite voice.

"Bed nine," one of them said.

I walked along past a couple of bays and then saw, in a

corner, by a window, Tyler sitting in an armchair by a bed. His eyes were closed, his head leaning against one of the wings of the chair. I was shocked at the sight of him. He was wearing a dark red dressing gown and against it his face was a milky colour. Down one side of his face was a ragged wound about five centimetres long. It had been stitched but was stained with yellow. There was a drip attached to his arm. The dressing gown was open at the front and I could see bandaging around his chest. He had pyjama bottoms on and his foot, in a plaster, was up on a stool in front of him.

He wasn't the same lad I had seen on Friday.

He opened his eyes and saw me. He moved around in the chair, his face flickering with pain as he tried to sit upright. He didn't smile. I stepped across and picked up a chair and carried it closer. Leaving a space between us, I put it down and sat on it, crossing my legs tightly at the knee, folding my arms, waiting to see what he had to say.

There was silence. Then he spoke. "Hi, Tyler," he said, imitating me, his voice a little raspy. "How are you? How are you feeling? It's so nice to see you!"

I shifted about on the chair, feeling awkward.

"I was going to ask. How are you?" I said, coughing lightly to clear my throat.

"Not too good. I swallowed half the canal."

I almost smiled. He almost smiled.

"You had an operation?"

He nodded and pointed to his foot.

"You don't look well," I said, stating the obvious.

"I don't feel well."

"What about your head?"

"Five stitches."

I looked at his bedside cabinet. Two books sat there, one on top of the other. They appeared brand new, as if someone had bought them as a gift. I angled my head to see what they were. One was by a writer whose name I didn't recognize but the other was by George Orwell.

"Still reading George Orwell?" I said, with a forced smile.

He gave a shrug, dismissing the subject. I felt idiotic, as though I'd misread what was important. He'd almost died and I was talking about books. *Stupid, stupid.*

I lowered my voice. "Who attacked you?"

His eyes met mine. They were dark against his pale skin and seemed lifeless. He shook his head and grimaced with pain, his hand grabbing his side. He gestured for me to move closer. I edged the chair along the floor. I thought he was going to say something but his eyes were closed. He looked as though any words might be too much effort.

"Was it anything to do with . . . last Christmas?" I said, looking round as if someone might be listening.

He opened his eyes.

"Was it Billy Rob?"

He leaned forward, reached his arm out gingerly and took my hand. He gripped it and pulled it towards him. I looked round the bay, embarrassed.

"I need you to do something for me, Ashe. This is really important."

He was clinging to my hand. His skin was hot, fiery. I let my hand soften and moved closer to him. I focused on the bandages round his chest. They looked as though they were squeezing the breath out of him.

"I'm so glad you came," he said. "You don't know how grateful I am."

I felt bad. The previous day I had refused to come and he had had to send me a handwritten note to remind me that I owed him something. I shouldn't have made him do that. It was like begging.

He seemed to be making a huge effort to speak.

"I'm in a lot of trouble," he said, lowering his voice.

I frowned.

"What happened to me the other night was punishment. It could get worse and I need some help and I don't know who to turn to."

"What's wrong?"

"I can't tell you because it might be dangerous. That's why I have to ask you to do something for me without telling anyone else. Not a soul. Not Beth, not your brother. Not Jimmy. No one."

"What?" I said. "Is it illegal? To do with drugs?"

He shook his head.

"What is it about? What's *happened* to you?"

"I can't say. I can't answer. It's better if I don't," he said, leaning forward in the chair, his hand holding mine tightly, too tightly.

"I will help, course I will. But don't you think you should talk to the police?"

He shook his head. "Please, Ashe, you don't know how dangerous these people are. . ."

"Billy Rob? Is it Billy Rob?"

I pictured Billy Rob. I'd seen him around recently, in the Drake. He always had a suit on no matter what the weather was. He stood out from the crowd in the pub or in the street. Maybe that was precisely why he wore one.

The sound of a trolley approaching made us both look round. A male nurse was smiling in Tyler's direction. He had spiked black hair and a tiny beard on his chin like an arrowhead.

"Ready for your meds, Mr Harrington?" he said, in a gruff voice, as though he had a frog in his throat.

Tyler let go of my hand and flopped back in the armchair.

"I'll go out," I said, standing up.

"No, don't," he said.

"Go for five minutes," the nurse said, "then you can have him back. All to yourself. This is what you need, young Mr Harrington. A pretty girlfriend to keep you out of trouble."

"Five minutes, then come back?" Tyler said.

I walked away. I heard the sound of the nurse pulling the curtain round the bed. I went out of the ward and stood in the corridor by a window. I was agitated. I made myself calm down.

How could this have happened?

A year before things had been so different. Then I'd been swept along on some kind of mad ride. The

40

afternoons at his house had started with coffee, crisps, a movie or some music, but they'd ended up with us both lying on his bed entangled in each other's clothes. It had only taken a few days for me to develop a powerful longing for him. It felt like *love*. I never said anything to him and he never mentioned the word to me, but I had such a yearning to be with him, to touch him, to talk to him, to lie with him. I sat my mocks and answered the questions and wrote the essays and ticked the multiple choice sheets and then I closed my eyes and ran my fingertips back and forth across my lips and thought about being in his room, hot and unsettled, watching the darkness thicken outside.

It was during one of those afternoons that we had the conversation about drugs. He'd been reading a book called *The Drug War and Capitalism*. I'd been trying to distract him. In the end I'd lifted his glasses off and made him look at me. Then the book had ended up on the floor. Afterwards I asked him the question that had been on my mind.

"Do you deal drugs?"

"No," he said, sitting back on a pillow, lifting his glasses off the bedside table. "I just pick up some smoke for my mates."

"So, you sell it to them?"

"No!"

"But they give you money for it?"

"Yes. Only what it costs. I don't make any profit on it."

"Still. . ."

"Look, a few of my mates like a couple of roll-ups. They're the nervous types. They won't go and buy it for themselves. They're not worldly wise, you know what I mean?"

I didn't answer. I opened Tyler's drawer and pulled out a hairbrush and started to brush my hair with it.

"They're too worried about getting caught, whatever, so I pick their stuff for them. I talk to Billy Rob and he gives me what I want, no more no less. I pay for it. Then I give it to my mates and they give me what they owe me."

"Billy Rob?" I said.

"He's this man – well, late twenties. He's the son of Marty Robertson, this guy I do courier work for."

"Why's he called Billy Rob?"

"He used to nick stuff when he was at school and his dad's name is Robertson so some bright spark coined the name and it stuck. He's a prat, always trying to show off to his dad, but he's easy to find and he's always got stuff for sale."

"Was he in the pub that night of my mum's party?"

"That's him. Always smartly dressed. A prat all the same."

I remembered the young man in the suit I'd seen in the smokers' area of the pub on the night of my mum's birthday party.

"He's a dealer. But I am *definitely* not a dealer."

I thought for a minute. "But if the police caught you, you'd get charged."

"Probably, but that's just a technicality. Look, if you wanted, say, a can of baked beans. . ."

"I don't want a can of baked beans," I said, turning round and using Tyler's brush on his hair.

"But if you did and you knew someone who was going to the supermarket and they were getting beans already, you might say to them, get me a can of beans and I'll give you the money when you get back."

"I don't like baked beans," I said, kneeling up on the bed, pulling the brush through Tyler's hair.

"Then when they get back from the supermarket with the baked beans, then you'd take yours and give them the money. They're not dealing baked beans. They're just doing you a favour."

But we stopped talking then because Tyler took the brush out of my hand and tossed it away, pushing me on the bed and holding me down while counting, the way they did on wrestling matches.

Three weeks. At the time it seemed longer. When we were together the hours stretched out, the minutes ticking slowly by, the afternoon darkness falling in slow motion. The time in between our meetings raced by and I was impatient to get my coat, leave the house and run round the streets to his room. I was like a crazy girl.

The hospital seemed very quiet. All the noises sounded as though they were far away in the distance: heels walking along a floor, wheels moving, creaking doors, female voices, male voices, babies crying. It felt like I was a long way from everyone. I looked out of the window.

Down below the traffic was stationary as ever. The sky was cloudy and it seemed as though it was getting dark even though it was before three.

What had happened to Tyler?

The ward door opened suddenly and it was the male nurse with the trolley. He didn't notice me standing there and just passed by.

I could leave. I could walk back to the lift. Being close to Tyler again was *dangerous* for me. Not because of Billy Rob but because of my bruised feelings. The truth was I wasn't over him. If I went back into the ward and did what he asked I would be vulnerable, easily hurt.

He was badly injured, though. He needed help and he had asked me. He hadn't asked his new girlfriend or Jimmy. He'd turned to *me*. On my letter he'd written *You owe me* and it was true. I had to help him whatever it cost me. I had to take my chances.

I turned and went back into the ward.

SIX

Tyler was still in the armchair. On the bedside cabinet was a small plastic vial which contained three tablets. One was blue and red, the other two chalky white. A glass of water sat next to them. On Tyler's drip was a fresh plastic bag of clear liquid.

The ward was uncomfortably warm. I unzipped my jacket as a couple of nurses burst into laughter at the desk. He started speaking as soon as I sat down.

"Thanks for coming back."

I smiled at him. I wanted to put my hand out and hold his, as we had been before the nurse came, but I was too shy. My chair was a little further back and I felt distanced from him. I leaned forward to hear him.

"I need you to go to my house when my parents are out. You can get something for me."

"What?"

"There's an envelope there. It's got some stuff in it that I don't want anyone else to find."

"What is it?"

"I can't tell you. You don't need to know. You just need to go to my house and get it."

He turned slowly, his face stiffening with pain. He

pulled open the drawer of the bedside cabinet and fished out a key ring.

"Here," he said.

"I thought you didn't live there any more?"

"It's still my *house*."

"What about your mum and dad?"

"Go tonight between seven and eight. They'll be up here visiting me. Look on the drive. If the red Nissan's not there it means they've left."

He was holding the key out but I hadn't taken it.

"There's no one else I can ask. It has to be someone I can trust."

"What about Jimmy?"

"Jimmy knows too many of the people I know. It would put him in an awkward position."

The key was still hanging between us. He offered it to me again. Why hadn't he asked the new girl that I'd seen him with? I had a sudden image of her in my head ruffling his hair as he sat beside her in the car. It made my throat ache.

"You're the only person who I can trust to do this."

I took the key from him. He looked relieved.

"When you get into the house, go up to my bedroom. Go to my wardrobe. Move the chair that's beside it and look behind. There's a padded envelope wedged there."

"You want me to bring it here?"

"No, no. You need to *hide* the envelope. It's A4 size. Can you do that?"

I nodded.

"There's nothing illegal in the envelope. You have to trust me on that and you have to promise me you won't open it and you absolutely won't give it to anyone else. When I get out of here I have some people to see and then I'll get the envelope from you."

He seemed out of breath. He leaned across and took my hand again, the one that held his key.

"This is so important, Ashe. *Promise* me you'll do it."

"I will. *I will*."

"Thanks," he said, letting go of my hand, flopping back on the chair, looking worn out, as if he'd just run five kilometres.

"You helped me out last Christmas. . ."

"No. Ssh. . ." he said, shaking his head. "No need to talk about that. That's done. That's over."

"I was grateful."

"I know you were."

"I owe you."

I hadn't meant to say the words but they just came out.

"I know that. But I think you would have done this even if you hadn't owed me anything. Because you liked me once," he said.

"I did," I said. It was on the tip of my tongue to add *I never stopped liking you.*

"Will you come and see me again? After you've got the envelope?"

I nodded. He seemed to relax for the first time. He

closed his eyes and sat very still. I got up and left, putting his house keys into my pocket.

When I got home Beth was there. She was in the kitchen with Dan. He had made her a hot drink and they were sitting across the table from each other.

"Want one?" he said to me, pointing at a steaming mug.

I shook my head.

"You all right?" Beth said. "You weren't in Business Studies. Someone said you'd gone home ill?"

"I was just feeling a bit fed up. I went for a walk."

"In this weather?"

"It's not that cold," I said.

"Dan's been working on some songs. He played one for me."

"Great," I said, distractedly.

"Dan says I might be able to sing one. To help him make a demo."

"You can't sing!" I said, but even as the words came out I knew I was wrong. Beth was a good singer. I'd heard her at school.

"We're going to do it at the weekend," Beth said.

Dan nodded pleasantly.

"Just got to go upstairs and get a couple of things," I said.

"You want me to come?" Beth said, uncertainly.

"No, you keep Dan company."

I went upstairs and sat on my bed, full of trepidation. I pulled my knees up to my chest and thought about Tyler sitting in the hospital chair, battered and helpless. It made me feel tearful. A while later I heard Beth coming up the stairs. I blew my nose and looked in the mirror to make sure that my face wasn't red.

"I'm just off now," Beth said. "By the way, Mum said that Tyler's on the mend. I thought you'd want to know."

I nodded.

"You know what? Today is the first day since last Saturday that you haven't asked me about him! See you tomorrow? At the bus stop?"

"OK."

"Listen, you don't mind me spending a bit of time with Dan?"

"Course not," I said.

Later I thought about Beth's love life. Like mine, it wasn't much to speak about. She had had a few lads who'd been interested and she'd spent a bit of time with them, gone to parties, gone for walks, seen movies, been round their houses when their parents were out. There'd been no one special for her, though. She was often keen in the lead-up to seeing someone, but after a few days or a week she always managed to find a reason not to bother. *He talked too much about football. He was too tall. His clothes smelled of nicotine.* When she'd decided it was no good she always seemed to perk up. She and I were comfortable together. I had been the same. Apart from Tyler there was no one else that I had really liked. I had tried but really it was too much effort. Sitting with a fixed smile on my face, pretending to have seen the films they were talking about, being knowledgeable about the bands they liked. It was a relief to get back to spending time with Beth again.

I stayed in my room for a while looking at schoolwork. From time to time I glanced up at the clock. The time crept forward. I went on to Facebook and then tried to do some reading. I heard Dan come up the stairs and he poked his head round my door.

"Sis, I bought something for you."

I looked up. He was holding a key fob in the air. It looked like it had a gold lipstick attached to it. I frowned.

"It's a memory stick. You said you were always losing them so I got this."

He picked up my bunch of keys from the desk and threaded it on to the ring.

"There! Don't say I don't buy anything for you."

He held the keys up. In among the other silly stuff hung this gold memory stick. I reached out for it, taken with its neatness and its shiny surface.

"Don't forget to use it, though. Just save your essays and notes. Important stuff. That way it doesn't matter if your laptop crashes," he said, going out of the room.

"Doesn't help me with Facebook," I called, "or my emails!"

He didn't answer and I smiled at his thoughtfulness.

My mum came in from work after five and I could smell food from downstairs. I didn't feel hungry but I went down to the kitchen anyway. My mum spooned me out some stew and a jacket potato and I sat at the kitchen table eating it.

"Has Dan said anything to you about not going back to university?" my mum said.

I shrugged.

"I thought I'd suggest some other university websites. There are masses of other courses."

I wanted to say, *Mum, leave him alone. Let him sort himself out*. But I didn't.

"You going out tonight?"

I nodded. "I just have to pop out for half an hour later. I've got to give Beth something."

"I'll give you a lift, if you like."

"No, that's OK. I don't mind the walk. Good exercise."

My mum gave a sigh. "Well, nobody needs me, then!" She was smiling as she said it but I could see by the shape of her mouth that she meant it.

I managed to finish most of my stew and I went back upstairs. I got changed into my jeans and a warm top and my trainers. I emptied out an old rucksack and sorted out my phone, making sure it was on silent. When I saw that the time was 18:32, I began to get anxious. I put Tyler's keys into the zip pocket at the front of my rucksack. Then, without saying anything to Dan, I went downstairs. Mum was watching television and I waved and went out into the street.

There was nothing for me to be nervous about. I was just collecting something for Tyler. Five minutes was all it would take. I had to do it. I owed him.

SEVEN

The red Nissan was in the drive. It was five past seven and for some reason it was still there even though Tyler had said that his mum and dad would be visiting him between seven and eight. I stood across the road looking at his house. I didn't know what to do. It was a residential street with cars parked bumper to bumper. I looked out of place and in any case I just couldn't stand there staring at the house waiting for them to come out and get in their car.

But I couldn't not go in and get the envelope. I'd said I would.

I decided to walk up the street to the end where there was a newsagent's. I could go in and buy a chocolate bar. Then I would walk back down. It would take about ten minutes in all and by that time his parents might have gone to the hospital. At least I'd be doing something.

I headed off, my footsteps slow and steady, just killing time.

I'd walked up and down Tyler's street many times during those days a year before. It was always in the afternoon when his mum and dad were at work. I was usually on my way home from a mock exam or last-minute revision class. I was wearing my uniform and carrying my rucksack. Once inside his house I took my tie and my shoes off and settled down in his room to listen to music or watch a DVD or scoot about on the internet. We had the house to ourselves but we hardly ever went out of his room. Tyler had everything we needed in there. Occasionally he went downstairs to get drinks or snacks and when he came back up he was followed by the cat, a thin grey creature with eyes like black beads. It spent ages tiptoeing around the room before it found a place to settle. *Say hello to Sophia*, Tyler had said.

It was as if we were in our own little world.

Those afternoons were wrapped in shadows. The daylight shrunk before our eyes. The wall lamps in his room gave out a weak glow and Tyler's face was always half in shade. It seemed, when we were sitting or lying in his room, that it was late at night. Sometimes the cat, Sophia, would lift her head up and stare at me for a while. We often ended up talking in whispers even though there was no one else in the house. When I left (always before his mum and dad got home from work) the street seemed too busy, too noisy. It was like waking up and being thrust out into the world.

We hadn't only been together in his house. We went out to a pub a couple of times and we went to see a silly Christmas film. We went for a pizza down at Canary Wharf, this giant shopping centre underneath all the skyscrapers that held banks and financial institutions. And we went to a party. The nicest times were in his room, though, luxuriating in the heat and the semi-darkness, listening to music and talking (and doing other *stuff* as well). It gave me a chance to ask him about himself.

"Why did you drop out of school?"

"I was asked to leave."

"They expelled you?"

He shook his head. "They asked me to give up my place in sixth form to a student who really wanted it."

"And you didn't want it?" I said, looking at the pile of books on his bedside table.

"No."

I reached out and picked up a book. It was *1984* by George Orwell. Underneath it was another by the same author, *Down and Out in Paris and London*.

"More George Orwell."

"I like him. I've read a couple of his books."

"Funny. I didn't think boys *read* fiction voluntarily."

"Ah! Orwell writes non-fiction as well as fiction. He's brilliant. If we'd done more stuff like that at school I might have turned up now and then."

I put the book back on the pile. When I looked up, Tyler was holding my bunch of keys. He looked quizzical.

"What is this?" he said. "How many keys do you need?"

"There are only three keys there. My two front door keys and my school locker key. The rest are key fobs. When I was younger I collected them. I should get rid of a few of them really, but. . ."

The key fobs hung brightly from the ring; a large silver heart hung lowest, surrounded by a mini Eiffel Tower, a football, my initial A and several smaller charms, which glittered in the half-light.

"What, are you ten years old?" he said.

"I like them!" I said, grabbing the bunch from his hand.

I dropped them on the floor beside his bed alongside my school jacket, rucksack and shoes. They sat there amid my younger self. Lying on the bed, beside him, I changed the subject briskly.

"So what are you doing now that you're not at school?"

"I do bits and pieces."

"Like what? Selling drugs?"

"I told you I don't sell drugs! I do some courier work for Marty Robertson. He has this business, Foneswapshop, near Mile End station? They sell phones but do a lot of business online and if it's in London it's actually quicker and cheaper for someone to courier the goods around on the tube. I don't do it all the time. Just when there's work."

"But not now?"

"Some early-morning stuff. While you're still putting your school uniform on."

"Don't you want a proper job? A career?"

"Yeah. That's why I'm starting at college next year. I'm going to finish my A levels."

"So you wasted a year?"

"No. I had to find out for myself that it was the school I hated and not *learning*. What is this? The third degree?"

"Just curious."

He leaned across me on the bed and slid his fingers under my top.

"Yeah, well, there're a few things that I'm just curious about as well."

But I rolled away. It was time to go. I pulled my stuff together and put my coat on and went out into the real world. That was how it was. When I think of those three weeks, I don't think about going to Canary Wharf, I think of those afternoons, in his room, in our own little world.

It all changed, though. Within a few days it all fell apart.

All because of my brother Dan.

The newsagent's was open. Outside were a bunch of kids I recognized from a lower year at my school. I didn't acknowledge them but a couple of them looked at me and nudged each other. I went into the shop and bought a chocolate bar and hung around for a minute looking at the magazine covers. Then I walked back out and strode along the road. I'd been a while, I was sure, and when I got back to Tyler's house I was relieved to see the red Nissan gone and the house in darkness.

I got the key out of my pocket. I instantly felt guilty. Up to that point I'd just been doing a favour for someone, but now I was actually breaking into a house without the owner's permission. I walked across the road and with a quick look up and down the street I went up the front path and put the key in the door. It opened and I stepped inside and closed it behind me.

It was pitch dark. I didn't turn the light on; I waited until my eyes had adjusted and I went slowly up the stairs, my foot feeling each stair out carefully. When I got to the landing I saw a tiny blue light blinking on and off from the bathroom. I stopped, but then I realized what it was. An electric toothbrush was recharging.

I felt my way along the landing and pushed at Tyler's room door. I went inside and closed it behind me. Tyler's curtains were open and there was light from outside. I could see a half moon in the sky and it meant that the area around the window was semi-bright. I could see the outline of all the things in the room: the bed, the chest of drawers, the desk, the armchair, the wardrobe. It was tidy, not at all the way it had been when I'd visited. There was nothing out of place. It was a reminder that Tyler hadn't lived there for a long time. The bedside clock showed 19:23.

I moved across the room to the armchair by the wardrobe. I edged it away, giving myself enough room to step up close to the side. I ran my fingers along the corner that was next to the wall. About halfway down I felt something. I probed further and felt the corner of the envelope. It was wedged.

I leaned against the wardrobe, trying stupidly to move it a couple of centimetres, but it was too heavy. I had to slide two fingers in and try to pluck the corner of the envelope. It took a few moments but then I did get hold of it. I pulled very carefully, nervous of losing my grip and of it falling further back in behind the immovable piece of furniture. I kept my arm steady and felt it coming, moving towards me. It snagged at one point, as though it was caught on a splinter or a nail, but I held it firm and gave a sudden pull and it came, the corner of it visible now so that I could use the fingers of both hands to edge and pull at it until it came out.

It was an A4-size padded envelope. I felt around it and visualized the edge of paper or cardboard inside as well as a small oblong shape: a memory stick, perhaps. There was also something square down one end. It felt like a CD. The envelope was fastened at the top, firmly sellotaped. There was no name or address or writing of any kind on the outside.

I allowed myself to breathe easily and let my shoulders move to get rid of the stiffness and tension. I stepped away from the wardrobe and edged the armchair back. Then I put the envelope into my rucksack and zipped it up. I looked at the clock. 19:32. It was time to go. I walked across to the door and had a quick look round to make sure that there was no sign that anyone had been there.

I went out of the room and headed along the landing. I was just about to go downstairs when I heard a noise. I stood very still for a moment, listening hard. There was no further sound. I thought it must have come from outside. I walked down a few stairs.

Then I heard it again. I paused, my jaw tight with anxiety. It was a banging sound. Like a door closing at the back of the house. I didn't breathe. I clutched the rucksack and waited to hear footsteps or the sound of a voice. I expected the light to come on and for a second I felt my stomach drop.

But there was nothing.

I waited.

Sophia padded along the downstairs hallway. She must have come into the house through the cat flap. That had been the noise I heard. I felt myself loosen up, my muscles softening. I made a *Huh!* sound which seemed uncomfortably loud in the empty house. Sophia spun around. She stared at me for a few seconds, seemingly unconcerned by my presence, but then she shot off back towards the kitchen. Seconds later I heard the cat flap again.

I walked on downstairs. Then I left Tyler's house, taking care that no one was out in the street as I slipped out the front door.

EIGHT

When I got home I headed for my room.

I could hear the television blaring from the living room and as I went upstairs the noise of Dan's music filled the landing. The sounds mingled and made me feel normal again. It had just gone eight. I'd done what Tyler asked me to do and there had been no problems. The envelope that I had in my rucksack was innocent enough: buff coloured, padded, blank; the type you bought in W H Smiths. Nothing for me to get worried about. I was just holding it for a friend.

I put the envelope on the top shelf of my wardrobe and covered it with some summer T-shirts and skirts. My keys were rattling in my pocket, so I took them out and threw them on the bed. Then I remembered Tyler's keys. I took them out of my rucksack and put them on my bedside cabinet. The next day I intended to go to the hospital and give them back to him.

I sat down on my bed, the strains of Dan's music seeping through the wall. I picked up my remote and pointed it at the telly in the corner of my room. I flicked about from programme to programme. In the end I turned it off just at the moment that Dan's music went off. I could hear Dan talking on the phone to someone. A few seconds later he came out of his room and gave a little knock on my door.

"I'm just going to the pub for a drink with some mates. Do you want to come?"

I shook my head.

"Have you said anything about university to Mum yet?" I said.

"Nope," he said.

"When will you?"

"I'm going to wait her out. She'll raise the subject soon, don't you worry. See you!"

And he went. I heard him humming as he skipped down the stairs.

There was a definite cockiness about him since he'd returned from university. He seemed completely at ease with the fact that he had just given up on his degree and had decided to make his own decisions. I wondered how Mum was going to take this new Dan.

How different from a year before. Then he had fallen apart.

In the weeks after Mum's fiftieth I'd hardly noticed Dan. In any case we'd been a little distant from each other for a while. He had his mates, I had mine. Since the party I'd been doing my exams and seeing Tyler. When I was at home I was in my room doing revision or having endless phone calls with Beth, who was telling me about her mum's hospital stay and the drama about whether or not the baby would be all right. I listened to it in a distracted way, trying to reassure Beth but hurrying her off the phone so that I could just be by myself and think about Tyler.

My brother Dan was not on my radar.

Then, on the Saturday night when Tyler and I went to a party, Dan turned up with his mates. He spoke to me briefly, but the rest of the evening he was out in the kitchen or among some of the smokers in the back garden. Me and Tyler left early and I went home and went to bed a little worse for the cans of beer I'd drunk. I went to sleep quickly but woke up later with a dry mouth and a headache. It was almost three o'clock when I heard Dan coming in, stumbling up the stairs. I went out on to the landing, shushing him. He was completely drunk, his eyelids heavy, his face a little dazed. He had mud on the shoulder of his jacket and I guessed that he'd fallen over on his way home.

He looked miserable.

"Come on," I whispered, taking hold of his arm.

He staggered towards his bed. He pulled the duvet back and fell on to the mattress without getting undressed. I covered him up, leaving only his boots sticking out. I squatted down and undid the laces and pulled them off. I opened his wardrobe door and placed the boots in.

Then I found the drugs.

The first thing I saw was an electronic scale, the kind you might find in a kitchen. I frowned, wondering what it was doing in the bottom of Dan's wardrobe. Next to it were packs and packs of tiny plastic bags. They were less than five centimetres square and had one edge that fastened. There were hundreds, it seemed.

I sat down on the floor. Behind me Dan was sleeping soundly.

I'd seen these kinds of bags around. They held tablets or dope or other drugs. They were bought and sold in school or passed around at parties. I'd even seen some girls with them that night, giggling and running upstairs to the loo to take whatever it was they'd got hold of.

And Dan had them.

I couldn't get this straight in my head. Why did my brother have this stuff? I reached across and moved the scale and the packs of bags and there, underneath, was a toiletries bag. I pulled it out and waited a second before unzipping it. Inside there were several fat plastic bags full of tablets and some dope.

I looked round at Dan.

Anger flared up inside me. How could he?

He was out cold and didn't look like he would be waking up for hours and hours, so I picked up the scale and the rest of the stuff and took it into my room. I dropped it all on my bed and stared at it for a few moments. Then I looked round and my eye settled on my old sports kit bag. It was gold and had glitter writing on it that said *Girl Power*. It was big enough to hold the stuff I'd found. I placed the things inside and zipped it up and shoved it on top of my wardrobe.

I didn't sleep for a long time.

Dan didn't surface until past midday the next day and

it was a couple of hours after that when he finally came into my room looking shocked and pale. He was wearing jeans and a T-shirt but his feet were bare and his hair was wet.

"What?" I said, angrily, hours and hours of tension and annoyance coming out in that one word.

"Where's my stuff?" he said in a hoarse whisper.

"What? Your drug-dealing equipment?"

"You don't know anything about it."

"No, I don't."

"I want the stuff back. It's not what you think. I owe someone. . ."

"Dealing drugs?"

"I'm not doing it out of choice."

"Then what?"

Dan looked around my room, his eyes settling on cupboards and drawers. He was looking for it.

"Where is it, Ashe? I have to have it back!"

"Why? Have you got to go out and sell it?"

"You don't know. . ."

"Where's the best place?" I said. "The Drake? The Feathers?"

These were the pubs that kids went to before parties and gigs.

"Or maybe you do the school run. Not at our school probably but round by the boys' comprehensive? Or what about the local primary? There might be good business to be done there!"

He turned away from me and looked as if he was going

to walk out of my room. My temper was up, though. I raised my voice.

"Or maybe you stand on the corner of Alexandra Drive. Just waiting for the customers to drive by."

He turned back. He looked awful. He sat on my bed with his elbows on his knees and his head in his hands.

Alexandra Drive was a road that divided a well-off area and an estate. All sorts of cars drove there and pulled up to buy drugs of one sort or another. A policeman who came to our school had talked about it. I'd seen it myself when Dad had picked me up from Beth's late one night. Sometimes they did business at a small roundabout at the top of Alexandra Drive. Cars simply drove round it, let their electric windows down and handed out the money while some young man handed in the plastic bags. At other times they bought and sold at the quiet end of the road near the park fence or down by the precinct. It just depended where the police were.

"I can't explain," he said, without looking up, "but I need that stuff back."

"I'm getting rid of it."

He shook his head. He was staring at the carpet, refusing to make eye contact with me.

"For all you know I've already dumped it down the toilet."

"Have you?" he said, looking up.

I shook my head.

His eyes were glassy, as if he was about to cry. It made

me wince. I hadn't seen him cry since he was a little boy. He pulled tissues out of his pocket and blew his nose.

"I have to sell the stuff," he said, pulling himself together, "because I've accidentally got myself into something."

"What, you mean you *tripped* into a drug dealer?"

"There's this guy, Billy Rob. He's always around the pubs and gigs. He's given me a lot of free stuff. Every time he saw me; a bit of dope, a few Es, some stronger stuff. He just gave it away like it was sweets. Whenever I saw him he said, *"Danny, my lad, I've got some stuff here for you and your mates."*

Billy Rob. The son of Marty Robertson, the man Tyler worked for.

"He was at Mum's birthday party. Downstairs, out in the smokers' area."

Dan nodded.

I thought of his smart suit. Everyone else had looked chilled to the bone but he stood smiling as if the cold couldn't touch him.

"How long have you been using this stuff?"

"I'm not *using* it. I'm not dependent on it. It's just recreational."

The word *recreational* made me think of children playing in a park, of swings and roundabouts and climbing frames.

"I know you smoke dope. Are you taking anything else?"

"Ashe, everyone has a bit of dope or tries some speed. Everyone does."

I thought of Tyler and his tins of baked beans.

"I don't! Beth doesn't!"

"Most kids do."

"I know loads of kids who don't."

"You think you do. It's easy to get. It's like picking up a chocolate bar in Tesco's. That's how easy it is. Or it seemed like that."

He stopped for a second.

"Now this guy, this Billy Rob, he says he wants me to *sell* it. That stuff you took from my room. He wants me to get new people to buy it. He says I owe him. Once I've sold *that* stuff, then we're clear."

"Tell him you won't. Tell him you'll go to the police."

"I can't."

"Has he threatened you?"

"Not exactly."

"Well, then!"

"It wasn't a threat so much. . ."

"What did he say?"

"He said that I didn't want to end up like Stuart Lister."

"Who's Stuart Lister?"

"Some kid who left school a couple of years ago. I didn't really know him but I saw him around. He was at a couple of gigs and parties."

"What happened to him?"

"He got run over."

"So?"

"It was a hit and run. He was on his way to work early

in the morning. No one saw the car that hit him but he died straight away."

"And this *Billy Rob* said this to you? As a threat?"

Dan nodded.

"You could go to the police with that. That's intimidation!"

"I'm not going to the police, Ashe. I'm going to sell this stuff and get Billy Rob off my back."

I had a bad feeling in my gut. "Then you're just as bad as them."

"Where is it, Ashe?" he said, standing up.

I pointed to the gold bag on the top of my wardrobe. He went across and got it down. Then, without a word, he left my room.

Now, a year later, Dan was out drinking with his friends. Drugs were a thing of the past with him. For Tyler it was different. Everyone knew what Tyler's business was.

I knew it most of all. It was why I broke it off with him.

NINE

The hospital was busy when I went in to see Tyler the next afternoon. There were numbers of visitors standing in little groups in the corridor, some small children running around. I edged around them, taking care not to step on anyone. I had Tyler's keys in my rucksack. I'd put them inside an envelope which held a get-well card. I couldn't be sure he would be on his own, but still I wanted to hand them over and let him know, by my presence, that everything was all right. His envelope was tucked safely away in my wardrobe.

I wasn't intending to stay long. I'd told Beth to come round my house after school. I'd been a bit distant from her over the last couple of days and I wanted to get things back to normal.

I pushed the ward doors open and went across to the alcohol rub dispenser and cleaned my hands. I passed the male nurse with the little beard. I gave him a smile but he looked at me in a distant way, as if he didn't remember who I was. I got to the bay where Tyler had been the previous day but he wasn't there. The bed he had been in was stripped and remade as if waiting for a new patient. I looked around. I thought that perhaps his bed had been moved to another bay so I walked around the whole ward. Then I wondered if he'd been moved to another ward entirely. I looked for the male nurse and found him in the day room straightening chairs and tidying newspapers.

He remembered me then.

"You're the girl who visited Tyler Harrington yesterday."

I nodded.

"You've missed him," he said, walking out of the room towards the nurses' station. "He went home this morning. Against doctor's orders."

I followed him.

"Went home?"

I pictured Tyler from the previous day. He'd been a grey colour, breathless, his foot in plaster. He hadn't looked as though he could walk to the end of the ward, let alone out of the hospital and home.

"Afraid so," he said, touching his beard, pulling it into a point at his jaw. "It seems as though he woke up this morning and decided he wanted to go home. I wasn't on duty, but he asked a nurse if she could help him get dressed. It was about eight? She put a call out for the duty doctor. If a patient wants to go home before the doctor agrees, they have to sign certain forms, and he needed his meds, antibiotics, painkillers, and so on."

"Wasn't he on a drip?"

"That came off late last night."

"So the hospital let him go home?"

"No, no. That's what I'm telling you. The nurse helped him get dressed. All he had to do was wait to see the doctor, get his meds and sign the release forms. But he didn't wait."

"How do you mean?"

"One minute he was sitting on his bed. The next minute he was gone."

"Did his mum and dad come for him?"

"I don't know. One of the other nurses said she thought she saw him being pushed out of the ward in a wheelchair by a man in a suit. Anyway, he's a very naughty boy. He left the hospital without signing himself out and he's got no meds so it's given us a few headaches."

Phones were ringing and the nurse was looking round in a harassed way. A man *in a suit* was wheeling Tyler in a wheelchair. It could have been his dad. His dad could have come early and picked his son up. But wouldn't he have waited to sign the release forms? And get the medication that Tyler needed?

"I expect it'll turn out that he'd had enough of nurses and doctors telling him what to do. When you see him, you tell him that we are very annoyed with him!"

"Have you contacted his parents?"

"I spoke to his mother and asked about where to send his meds, but she doesn't know where he is. He doesn't live with his parents. She thinks he may have gone to stay with a friend. She sounded upset."

It *couldn't* have been his dad who wheeled him out if his mum didn't know where he was.

"I must get on," he said and backed away from me towards the desk. In a second he had a telephone at his ear and was speaking rapidly into the mouthpiece. There was more I wanted to ask but he had cut away from me. The ward seemed to be moving swiftly round me. A nurse with a trolley of laundry passed by; another with a blood pressure monitor dashed the other way. A porter was at a bed helping a man into a wheelchair. A group of people in regular clothes with clipboards were talking in hushed tones. The nurse had finished his phone call and had headed off down the other end of the ward. I felt stranded. I didn't know what to do.

Tyler had gone home? It seemed unlikely. He hadn't waited to get signed out and he had no medication. A man in a suit had wheeled him out.

Was it *Billy Rob*?

There was nothing else for me to do but go home. I walked out of the hospital with a sense of foreboding. It was raining and windy. People were trying to hold umbrellas up but the rain was squally sucking them inside out. I walked out, letting the wind blow my hair this way and that. This was too much. Tyler was injured, bandaged up, his foot in a cast. He'd been tired after *talking* to me, let alone walking anywhere.

Who had taken him out of hospital?

Beth was already in my house. Mum said she was up in Dan's room. I could hear her talking as I went upstairs. I threw my coat and my rucksack on to my bed and went into Dan's room. Beth was sitting on the end of Dan's bed and Dan was at the computer.

"Beth, what's happened to Tyler?"

"Oh, Mum said he's discharged himself from hospital. My aunt's really upset. He did it without telling anyone. Why are you asking? How come you know he's out of hospital?"

"I went to visit him and he wasn't there," I said softly, hardly wanting to admit it.

"How come?" Beth said.

Dan had stopped what he was doing at the computer and looked round.

"I wanted to see how he was, that's all. No big deal. The nurse said that someone pushed him out of the ward in a wheelchair. He didn't even wait to get his medicines."

"Yeah," Beth said, "you know Tyler. He'd probably had enough of being fussed over."

"But he was in a mess! You told me yourself he got beaten up and thrown in the canal!" I said, with a squeak in my voice. "He had stitches in his head! A cast on his foot. They were worried about infection! Why would he leave the hospital?"

"With Tyler you just don't know. . ."

"Do you think someone might have taken him out? Against his will?"

"Why would anyone do that?"

"She's probably right, Ashe. Tyler just got fed up."

"But someone *attacked* him last Friday night. Maybe that someone has taken him out of hospital. Against his will!" I said, bursting with frustration.

"But wouldn't he have made a noise, shouted out?" Dan said. "Called for help? The hospital's full of people.

I'll bet that there was at least one copper somewhere around."

Why hadn't Tyler called out, cried for help? I didn't know. They were both looking expectantly at me.

"Oh, never mind," I said and walked out of Dan's room.

Moments later Beth followed me into my bedroom.

"Why are you getting so upset?"

"I just think it's odd. For him to just disappear like that."

"But Tyler's like that. He left his mum and dad's house in the summer and they never saw or heard from him for nearly *three weeks*. You should have seen how upset everyone was then!"

I remembered that time. Beth told me about it. It had seemed in character that Tyler should go off on his own. He'd been abroad, in Spain apparently, and hadn't bothered to let his mum and dad know. I'd gone to Crete for two weeks and when I came back she'd said that Tyler had turned up out of the blue just as her aunt and uncle had begun to think that he might have been dead. I'd shaken my head in a knowing and disapproving way. Tyler did bad things. People talked about it from time to time. I had learned to look as though I wasn't interested.

"It's like the family has got used to Tyler being in trouble. He spent sixteen weeks in prison!"

"I know, I'm sorry," I said.

"Is there something you haven't told me? About you and Tyler?"

Beth was staring hard at me, her eyes searching my face.

"I just, you know . . . I did like him. I still like him. I'm just. . ."

There was a moment's silence and I shrugged helplessly. Eventually she looked at her watch.

"I have to go," she said, glumly. "My mum's going out tonight so I've got to look after Sara. You could come back home with me. We could get a takeaway?"

I shook my head.

"I've got an essay to write," I said, glancing at my rucksack, which had been tossed on the bed.

"I'll ring you if I hear a single thing about Tyler," she said, looking at me in a quizzical way.

"Thanks," I said, softly.

I listened to her footsteps down the stairs and heard her calling out "Bye!" to my mum. Then I reached across for my rucksack, pulling the zip down. At the top was the envelope which held the get-well card and Tyler's keys. I put them on my bedside cabinet.

I started to unpack my books. I did have an essay to start. It was a week or so before the first draft was due in, but I could have planned it out, done some reading, made a few notes. I also had a talk to prepare and some research to do on the internet. But I didn't want to do any of it. I stood up and paced my room, standing at the door wondering how I was going to settle to anything with all this stuff going on.

I was involved.

I thought of Tyler sitting in the wheelchair, his face as pale as wax but for the cut and bruise by his eye. Someone had wheeled him out. Could it have been Jimmy? Jimmy didn't wear suits but could he have come in and got Tyler? Could it have been just bloody-mindedness about the release forms? Maybe they had just forgotten the medication? Was Tyler sitting in Jimmy's flat at that moment thinking of ringing the hospital to find out about his antibiotics and his painkillers?

I sat down on the edge of the bed full of anxiety. I dragged my coat back on. In one pocket was my travel card. In the other was my bunch of keys. I was going out. I had to find out what this was all about.

I had to find out where Tyler was.

TEN

I knew where Jimmy Connelly would be. His dad owned a second-hand furniture shop near Bethnal Green tube station and he worked there. I hopped off the bus and stood looking at it. It was called, imaginatively, Second-Hand Furniture. Someone had sprayed fake snow on the window that said *Merry Xmas*, the letters on *Xmas* getting smaller towards the end. Outside there was a mishmash of furniture sitting on the pavement; it looked like old IKEA stuff and a variety of old wooden chairs and a couple of television stands.

The light was fading even though it had just gone four. The wind had dropped but it was still raining. Some people were coming out of the tube station with heavy bags of what looked like Christmas shopping. It didn't feel like Christmas to me. All this stuff with Tyler had blotted it out.

I walked across the road, weaving through stationary cars, taking care that there were no bikes or mopeds speeding in between lanes. On the other side I sidestepped the furniture and looked inside. There was no one in the shop that I could see. I stepped inside the door and called out, "Hello?" There was no movement but I sensed someone behind me on the pavement.

"What can I do for you, miss?"

I turned round. It was a bald man in a puffa jacket.

"I'm looking for Jimmy?" I said.

The man smiled.

"You his girlfriend?" he said.

"No!" I said, louder than I meant to.

He passed me and walked into the shop. He must have been Jimmy's dad. He had the same thin frame and hunched way of standing.

"Is he around?"

"Gone out on an errand. Should be back soon. Why not wait for him? I've just put the kettle on. Grab a seat. There's plenty about."

He wasn't joking. Inside the shop there were headboards and tables and filing cabinets as well as a huge collection of chairs, some stacked and some sitting at odd angles. The shop was cold, as though it had no heating, and I guessed that was why Jimmy's dad had a heavy puffa jacket on. I sat down and pulled my coat around me, holding my hands together and slotting them between my thighs. I decided to wait. What was the point in going home again if Jimmy was due back soon? His dad was fiddling with a kettle and two mugs.

"I'm Tony, Jimmy's dad," he said, handing me a mug of tea.

"Hi," I said, awkwardly, "I'm Ashley."

Just then, a van pulled up outside, half on the pavement. There was loud music coming from it, something like ABBA, which stopped suddenly, making the place seem unnaturally silent. A second later a face appeared at the door of the shop.

"Tone? I got something for you."

"'Scuse me, Ashley," Tony said.

He put his mug down on a nearby filing cabinet and went outside. I cradled my tea, feeling the warmth coming off it. Through the window of the shop, in between the lettering of *Merry Xmas*, I could see the man opening the back door of the van pointing to something inside.

My mind went back to why I was there.

Why had Tyler left hospital? He'd said nothing to me about it the previous evening. In fact, he'd asked me to go and see him again. Had something spooked him so that he'd thought that being in hospital was no longer safe? Had he asked Jimmy Connelly to help him?

I took a mouthful of hot tea.

I remembered then how I had asked Tyler that very same thing a year before. *Will you help me?* I had said.

Hours after my brother had taken the drugs back from me I met Tyler by the canal and we sat on a wall near the old factories. I'd phoned him specially and said I needed to talk to him. It was a cold day and it was threatening to rain, the air damp against my face. Tyler had a parka on over a thick jumper. He had new trainers on, the laces loosely tied. He kept fiddling with them as I was talking.

"How could Dan get involved dealing drugs! I'm so angry at him!" I said.

Tyler didn't have anything funny to say. I'd explained it

all. I had expected him to be surprised but he wasn't. That made me feel worse somehow. He knew about drugs; he used them. He even bought them for his friends, for the shy types who were afraid of being arrested. My brother, it seemed, hadn't been shy about getting drugs.

"I told him to go to the police but he says this guy has threatened him and mentioned *Stuart Lister*. Did you know Stuart Lister? He was run over. It was a hit and run and Dan thinks that Billy Rob had something to do with it."

Tyler shrugged. "I don't know."

"What do you think Dan should do?" I finally said.

This was why I'd rung Tyler. This was why I'd poured it all out to him. Tyler was the only person I could actually talk to about this. I had thought that among all his jokiness and his knowledge about how to get drugs he might have a simple answer for me.

"Sell the stuff. Pay the debt to Billy Rob."

"He can't!"

"Why not?"

"Because he's not that kind of lad. He'd get caught. It would ruin his life. He might go to prison."

"It would take him a week. It would get Billy Rob off his back."

"Even if he did start to sell them he wouldn't finish it or he'd mess it up. He's not focused!"

"He's not focused enough to deal drugs? You don't need A levels, Ashe. Billy Rob just wants some new contacts. All Dan's got to do is sell some stuff around. He knows a lot of kids. There's a lot who want easy access to soft drugs."

"You don't know my brother."

"I was in the same form class as your brother for six years. I do know him. If he does it, then Billy Rob'll leave him alone. The thing about Billy Rob is that he'll lose face if Dan doesn't do it."

I remembered Billy Rob out in the smokers' area at the back of the Cheese and Ale pub. He had a wide smile and stood confidently amid the people there as if he were at a party and they were his friends.

"His dad, Marty Robertson, is a businessman. He puts the money up for his son to deal drugs. Then if Billy Rob makes any money it gets put through the books of Marty's company."

"How do you know this?"

"I don't. I'm guessing. I'm in and out of Marty's office and Billy Rob's always there; Marty must know what his son's up to. Billy Rob gets all his contacts among young people, that's all. He gives drugs to them and becomes mates with them. They think he's generous and fun and then after a while he starts to make demands on them. He gets them to sell it for him. He tried giving stuff to me once but I prefer to pay my way."

I gripped the edge of the wall with my fingers. The rain was spitting now. It pitted the water in the canal.

I was desperately disappointed. I had hoped that Tyler would have some solution, some idea which would straighten things out. I kept thinking of him talking about drugs as if they were cans of beans; it sounded sensible and clean, not dirty and dangerous.

Opposite, on the towpath, a solitary cyclist went past. He looked sideways at us and then continued on. He had small flashing lights on the back of his heels. They were bright like fairy lights and made me think of Christmas.

"Where can I find this guy, Billy Rob?" I said.

"Why?" Tyler said, frowning.

"I am going to go and see him. I can't leave this situation as it is. I'm going to give him back the drugs. And if he doesn't like it I'll threaten to go to the police."

Tyler sighed. His voice sounded mildly cross, as if he were a teacher giving me a pep talk.

"These people, like Billy Rob, like Marty Robertson, they don't get caught by the police. It's Dan's word against his. Dan's a student who's been messing round with dope and Es. Billy Rob will have a hundred excuses. He'll say he had the drugs for his own use and he gave them away. He'll make it sound like he's a saint."

"What about the thing he said about Stuart Lister?"

"What's Dan going to say to the police? Billy Rob said, *You don't want to end up like Stuart Lister*. That's a perfectly reasonable thing to say. Where's the crime in that?"

I listened with dismay. Inside I was realizing that Tyler had no easy fix for my brother.

"If you go and see Billy Rob he might well take the stuff back. He might not even argue with you. You'll think he's forgotten about it and months will go by and Dan'll be walking home late one night and some of Billy Rob's guys will jump him. No one will see it. No one will know it has anything to do with him. And then, in a year's time, he'll be saying to someone else, *You don't want to end up like Dan Littlewood*."

I couldn't speak. I felt full up with emotion.

"What am I going to do?"

"Why do you have to do anything? This is your brother's problem."

"That's why," I said, feeling my throat dry up, "because he is my brother and he's scared."

"Don't get upset," Tyler said.

But I couldn't help it. It was a big mess.

"You work for Marty Robertson. Would you go and see him? Explain it all to him?"

"What good would that do?"

"He knows you. He might listen to you. You could ask him to speak to his son. You could offer him some money," I said. "I've got over three hundred pounds in my building society book."

"Why don't you get some money off Dan?"

"I don't want to involve him."

"But you want to involve me?"

"My brother would mess it up. He's not sensible. He's not like you."

"God. No one's ever accused me of being sensible before."

"Please."

He was silent for a few moments, looking down at the ground.

"All right," he said, eventually. "I can't promise anything, though. You get the money out and the drugs and bring them to my house tomorrow afternoon. I've got an evening delivery tomorrow and I'll go and see him afterwards."

"Do you think he'll be OK with it?" I said, grabbing at straws.

"I don't know."

Now, a year later, I sat on a chair in Jimmy's dad's shop holding a cup of tea. Outside, Jimmy's dad was unloading more chairs from the back of a van. I looked around the crowded shop and wondered where he was going to put them. I stood up, stepped across to put my mug on the table and went to the door. I was struggling with the zip of my coat when I looked across the road to see Jimmy walking along. In moments he was across the road and standing in front of me.

"Your girlfriend's here!" his dad called and I rolled my eyes with irritation.

"What do you want, Ashe?" he said, walking past me into the shop.

"I want to know where Tyler is."

"Why ask me?"

"Someone took him out of hospital this morning," I said.

"So?"

"Was it you?"

"Why would I take him out of hospital?"

"Have you got any idea who might have taken him?"

"How should I know?" he said, angry all of a sudden.

"He's your friend. You know who he hangs around with. The people he works for. Where does he get his drugs from? That's how he makes his money, isn't it? You must know."

I was annoyed. I was worried about Tyler and Jimmy was being offish.

"Where is he, Jimmy?"

"Why are you bothered?" he said, picking up my used mug and taking it to a room at the back of the shop. "The other day you didn't even want to visit him in hospital."

From behind I could hear the sound of voices; Jimmy's dad and the other man were talking. I glanced round and saw them carrying in stacks of chairs.

"He asked you to come and you couldn't be bothered."

"I. . ."

"I don't know why Tyler ever wasted his time with you," Jimmy said. "Just a stupid schoolgirl."

"What's this got to do with anything?" I said, getting annoyed. "I just want to know what's happened to him. Why does it matter that he and I spent time together? I'm here as a *friend*. Not a girlfriend!"

"It does matter," he said.

"Why?"

"Because it's your fault he's in this trouble in the first place."

ELEVEN

We sat in Chaplin's Café. I had a can of Coke in front of me even though I didn't really want it. Jimmy had nothing. I was staring through the shop window at a silver Mini that was parked outside. The rain was forming on its surface like tiny bubbles.

"Why is it my fault that Tyler's in trouble?" I said, my tone a little softer now.

Jimmy had unzipped his puffa jacket. Underneath he had a thin T-shirt on. It made me feel cold to look at it.

"You remember you asked Tyler to speak to Marty Robinson? To get your brother out of trouble?"

I nodded. I'd been poring over it in my head just moments before. Yes, I remembered it, every anxious moment.

"He went to see Marty the next day."

"He told me," I said, irritably. "I gave him the money to pay Marty Robertson and he did. He sent me a text to say it was all right."

"He lied to you."

"What do you mean?"

"Marty wasn't interested in the money."

"What?"

I'd taken the gold bag from Dan's room early that morning while he was still asleep. I'd transferred the scale and the drugs paraphernalia into another bag. I left the house at the usual time and then went straight to the building society. As soon as it opened I'd emptied my building society account. Three hundred pounds. Fifteen twenty-pound notes. I'd gone round to Tyler's house and given him the money and bag.

Later that night I'd got a text from him.

Job done! XXXXXX

That was when I sent him the letter in the pink envelope.

Jimmy continued talking.

"He tried to persuade Robertson to take the money but he wouldn't."

"Why not?" I said.

"See," Jimmy said, taking a breath, "it was about his son. His son had told your brother to do something and Robertson didn't want to get involved. In case Billy Rob felt put out. Tyler tried but Robertson just told him to go and talk to Billy Rob."

"Tyler said he'd persuaded him. He said that Dan was in the clear."

"Yeah, he was in the clear, but only because Tyler told Billy Rob that he'd sell the drugs instead of Dan. That way Billy Rob didn't lose face. In fact, it was better for him. See, Billy Rob had been trying to get Tyler involved in selling for months. Tyler was a *challenge* to him. But Tyler wasn't interested and now Billy Rob had got him to do what he wanted. So your brother was like this tiny fish that he dropped back into the stream and Tyler was his big catch."

"Why didn't he tell me?" I said.

Jimmy shrugged. "Tyler thought he could sell the stuff quickly so that no one needed to know about it. He thought he could get your brother off the hook. All he had to do was shift some dope and Es."

"I can't believe it," I said, feeling winded, shocked.

"I don't know why you're so surprised. That was why you finished with him, wasn't it? You saw him selling drugs on Alexandra Drive?"

I nodded.

"You broke up with him because you said you didn't want anything to do with drug dealers."

I did remember it.

My dad was giving me a lift to Beth's house. I was going to see the new baby, who'd just arrived home from hospital. We'd had to drive the long way round through the backstreets because of roadworks. We were going slowly behind a learner driver and I was looking idly out of the window. I was in a good mood. I didn't even mind my dad playing his oldies at top volume and singing along in the car. It was four days after the night that I had found the drugs in Dan's room. I'd told Dan that it was all sorted out. He'd been wary at first but then said that he'd seen Billy Rob down at the pub and he'd given him the thumbs up. It was all over. I didn't mention the three hundred pounds because there was no point. That might have made Dan feel less good about it and I wanted it over and done with.

It was a couple of days before Christmas Eve and I had bought Tyler a present of a vintage West Ham shirt. I was going round later that night to give it to him.

Everything was going well.

Then I looked out of the window further up Alexandra Drive near the roundabout and saw a boy in a hooded top standing by the edge of the pavement. It gave me a chill because I was instantly reminded of all the anxiety I had had over Dan and his involvement with Billy Rob. The boy was in a shadowy recess between two shops.

A car pulled over to the side of the road and the boy came forward and I saw that it was Tyler. I couldn't believe it. I'd never seen him wear a hoodie. It was too ordinary for him, too much like what other kids wore. I wanted to smile but then the passenger window opened and Tyler reached into the car. I could see his profile. He pulled something out of a back pocket and handed it into the car. I could see him holding his hand out while the person in the car gave him something. It drove off then and Tyler stepped backwards into the shadow. We inched forward until we were alongside him but I looked away because I couldn't bear to see him.

He was selling. After all the times that he'd denied it. The things he'd said about tins of beans and getting stuff for mates. And here he was like any other street dealer waiting for cars to pull up and buy his wares. It gave me a leaden feeling in my chest.

Now a year later, it seemed that I had been mistaken.

Jimmy Connelly was staring at me.

"Wait," I said. "He was selling on *Alexandra Drive*. He told me that Billy Rob wanted kids to sell to their friends. So that they had new contacts. Why was he selling to people in their cars?"

"Billy Rob told him to. A couple of his kids had legged it and he needed someone there for two weeks. In any case Tyler didn't want to sell to his *mates*. Tyler had *principles*."

Jimmy made a huffing sound, as if he didn't approve of this.

"And that's when he was arrested. That's the price he paid for helping your brother out. You know the rest. He spent four months in prison. When he got out it was difficult to get a job. He drifted back towards Billy Rob. He got sucked into that crowd."

I let it sink in. All the things I had thought had been wrong.

"It changed Tyler. He wasn't the same person when he came out of prison. I hardly know him any more."

I drank my Coke even though it was too cold. Jimmy was staring at me but I found that I couldn't make eye contact. I was looking around the café. There were travel posters on the wall which showed sand dunes and pyramids. Over by the till there was a pot plant which was growing wildly, its shoots circling the pipes that went up the wall. The tables around us had tiny vases with paper flowers in them. Outside I could see the silver car starting up, its lights going on. Moments later it moved out into the traffic and was gone.

"Where is he now?" I said, after a few minutes' uncomfortable silence.

"I don't know. Maybe he decided that it was a good idea to disappear for a while."

"But who took him out of hospital?"

"He's got other mates, Ashe." Jimmy shrugged.

"You don't seem to care," I said.

"That's a laugh. Coming from you, who got him in this mess in the first place."

"You don't think that they'll do anything. . . The people who beat him up? Tyler said they were *punishing* him."

Jimmy didn't answer. Then he looked, for a moment, as if he had something he wanted to say.

"What?"

"Did Tyler. . . Did he ask. . .?"

"What?" I said.

"Oh never mind."

He zipped his jacket up, got up and left the café. I sat there until I'd drunk every drop of my Coke. Then I left.

TWELVE

Back at home, I held Tyler's envelope in my hand. It was past midnight and my house was quiet. My mum and dad were in bed, although I could hear sporadic voices, as though they were having a sleepy conversation. Dan was out.

The truth about last Christmas was hard to take. A whole year had gone by with me thinking one set of events had happened. As far as I'd been concerned, Tyler, who had told me that he only bought drugs for his nervous friends, had been lying. I had seen him doing it and felt betrayed. I'd given him up. I'd snatched my brother back from a dark road and then I built an invisible wall. On one side was the murky world of buying and selling little plastic bags of recreation; on the other side were me and my brother. We were clean. They were dirty. When Tyler was sent to prison I'd acted as though it had been expected. If I'd been upset or sad it was because of my memories of those days before I knew the truth about him.

But now the history of a whole year had been altered by what Jimmy had told me. Tyler had taken Dan's place to pay off Billy Rob and I'd known nothing about it.

I clasped the corners of the envelope. It was soft, puffed

out with stuffing. I wasn't supposed to look inside it, but things had changed. Tyler had been wheeled out of the hospital by a man in a suit. Neither his parents nor his friend knew where he was. As far as I was concerned he was in danger.

I pulled at the envelope but it was tightly fastened with sticky tape. I got up and rummaged around my desk and found a pair of scissors. I cut away at it. Then I edged the flap up. I upended it and watched as some things dropped out on to my bed.

A bunch of keys, a memory stick and a CD.

I picked each one up and looked at it intently, as if I could discern some clue from its appearance. The three keys were on a ring. There was a plastic key fob with a label, *Bryan*. There were two Chubb keys, one longer than the other. There was a Yale key as well. They all looked new, as though they'd been recently cut and had never been used. I wondered who Bryan was.

The memory stick was maroon. I decided to see what was on it. I stepped across to my desk and opened my laptop. A loud humming sound came on and I gritted my teeth, hoping it wouldn't disturb my mum and dad. I let it load up while I went back to the bed and looked at the CD. It was a band that Tyler liked. I remembered him playing it when I spent those afternoons in his room. I opened it and pulled out the insert of notes and lyrics. There was nothing behind it or between the pages. I wondered what its significance was. I was puzzled.

I picked up the memory stick. My laptop had loaded

and I went across and put it in the USB port. It took a few seconds but the box opened on the screen. There was a single icon. Photographs. I clicked on it and a series of pictures showed. There were ten of them and I guided the cursor on to the slide-show option. One photo filled the screen and stayed there for a few seconds before fading, and then another took its place. The first face I recognized was Billy Rob. He was standing next to a car. He was wearing his usual smart suit. I let the slide show continue, then clicked for it to play again. The main focus of the photos was the two men who were in the front seat of a car. I had no idea who these men were. One was about fifty with a heavy face. He was wearing black-framed glasses. The other was younger. He had short neat hair and a grin on his face. Billy Rob was in the first three photos. After that it was just the two men.

The photographer had taken the shots from in front of the car. Several of the pictures were close-ups and the faces could be clearly seen. The others were from a distance. The last two showed the passenger door opening and the younger one getting out. I looked at the older man again and wondered if it was Marty Robertson.

I didn't know.

I decided to save the pictures on to a file. I was tense for a minute in case my laptop crashed. It didn't, so I took the memory stick out, scooped up the keys and the mobile and was about to return it to the padded envelope when I noticed that there was something else inside. Something lightweight that had become wedged across the envelope. I used my fingers to edge it out. It was a photocopy of a news article. It looked like part of the front page of the *Metro*, a free newspaper. There was a headline and a photo.

> TEENAGER STABBED IN PARK ATTACK
> *Police suspect racist motives.*
> Twenty-two-year-old Joseph Lindsay was stabbed in an unprovoked attack in Woodberry Park on Tuesday night. Unconfirmed reports suggest this was a racist crime. The young man's body was found by a group of schoolchildren on Wednesday morning.

I read the rest of the article, which gave some details of where the boy went to school and what his friends had said. The police had issued a statement. *We will not tolerate racially motivated crimes. We have several lines of enquiry and hope to make an arrest soon. Our sympathies are with the family and friends of Joseph Lindsay.*

I looked at the article with confusion. What did it have to do with Tyler? Or the world he moved in? Who was Joseph Lindsay? Opening the envelope had raised more questions. I still didn't know what to do. I put everything back and replaced it on the high shelf in my wardrobe. In the morning I would ring Beth to see if there was any news about Tyler.

I got into bed and tossed and turned for ages. Tyler's words went over and over in my mind: *You have to promise me you won't open it and you absolutely won't give it to anyone else*. I'd broken my first promise and opened the envelope. It was a long time until I fell asleep.

When I woke up I felt heavy with fatigue. It was a struggle to get up out of bed. I had a bath and washed and dried my hair. Then I sorted out my books and my stuff for school. I had some breakfast, giving half-hearted answers to my mum when she tried to make conversation. Eventually, when I could wait no longer, I rang Beth. I was hoping she would say, *Yeah, he turned up at my aunt's last night. He's fine*.

"Any news on Tyler?" I said, when she answered.

"I haven't heard anything," she said.

"Could you do me a favour? Could you ring his mum and dad and check with them? It's really important."

"All right!" she said, sounding mildly peeved.

She rang me back about five minutes later.

"Hi," I said, anxiously.

"No news on Tyler. His mum doesn't know where he is. She said she loaned him a spare mobile when he was in hospital. Because his got lost in the canal? She's been ringing it ever since, but there's no answer. She's really upset."

"Oh."

"Ashe, what's going on?"

"I can't say right now," I said. "I've got something to do this morning, then I'll see you at school."

She rang off. I knew I would have to tell Beth about it soon.

But there was something I had to do first.

THIRTEEN

The police station was at the far end of the high street. I approached it slowly, still not completely sure that I was doing the right thing. The envelope was in my school rucksack, which was firmly on my back, as if I was hiking up a mountain. I had my hands shoved far down into my pockets. One hand was gripping my travel card; the other was fiddling with my key fobs.

Just before I left home I looked again at the photos on my computer screen, which I had saved from the memory stick. Two men talking in a car. I had it in my mind that the older man was Marty Robertson, but that was just a guess. The younger man's face was clear in the close-up shots and I didn't like his expression. He wasn't laughing, he was *grinning*, as though something had been said that mildly amused him. I couldn't help thinking that it was something nasty. I made up my mind that I didn't like either of these men. Then I looked to the side at the figure standing by the car. Billy Rob.

Had Tyler taken those photographs?

I couldn't answer either of these questions, so I closed the file and made my way out of the house.

I had to press a security button to gain entrance to the

police station. The reception area was small. Just a few chairs lined up against a wall, as though they hardly ever expected any members of the public to come in. A black girl was sitting on one of the chairs, her legs straight and sticking out. The toes of her shoes were fiercely pointed. I went past her and walked up to the counter. It was like a bank or building society with thick glass and computer screens. Only one position had someone standing at it, a thin female police officer who seemed to have no hair at all, so tightly was it pulled back off her face. She was staring at the computer screen and I felt awkward, as if I was interrupting her.

"Excuse me," I started.

"Be with you in a minute," she said, holding one finger up in the air as she moved the mouse and concentrated on the screen.

I stood awkwardly. I glanced round at the girl, who was tapping out a furious message on to a mobile. She was taking no notice of me and I wondered why I was so self-conscious.

"Yes?" the officer said, her face expressionless.

"I've come to talk to someone about my friend Tyler Harrington," I said, my words in a half whisper. "I'm worried about him."

"Who?" she said, using the kind of loud voice that was reserved for babies and foreigners.

"Tyler Harrington?" I said, loudly and slowly.

"What about him?"

"I think he may be missing?" I said, coughing lightly.

"Take a seat and I'll get someone to come and speak to you."

I took my rucksack off my back and sat down. I left a couple of spaces between me and the girl, who had now finished her text message and was lolling back against the wall, her eyes closed, listening to an iPod. I was tense. I'd never been in a police station before. The only thing I knew about the police was what I'd seen on the television. I had my arms around my rucksack. I was holding it tightly, as though I was afraid that someone was going to come and snatch it off me. I tried to relax and made myself think about what I would say.

Tyler Harrington is a friend of mine. He asked me to look after this envelope. . .

I wouldn't need to explain that I'd got it from his room after going into his house when his parents were out. That wasn't important. The contents of the envelope: that was what was important.

He asked me to look after this envelope and not to give it to anyone. He seemed anxious about it and now that he's gone missing I thought that the police should have it. . .

I felt movement from the side and saw the girl standing up. She gave the officer behind the counter a pouty look and then flounced off, her heels tapping on the floor. She stopped at the door and used the palm of her hand to hit the release button so that the door opened outwards. When she left, I looked over at the PC to see if her departure had been noticed, but the officer's expression was still deadpan, her fingers flying across the keyboard.

A man came out from a side door. He was wearing a zip-up jacket over his shirt and corduroy trousers. The jacket was hanging open and his belly poked out. He stepped towards the counter and spoke to the WPC.

"I thought you said there were two girls?"

The WPC shrugged. He looked puzzled. I wondered what he was talking about. I noticed his identity tag was on back to front.

"Excuse me, miss. I'm DI Mike Wren. How can I help you?" he said, patting his pockets and producing a watch which he looked at, then replaced.

I stood up. "My friend Tyler Harrington has gone missing."

"And you are?" he said.

"I'm a friend of his," I said. "Ashley Littlewood."

We were both standing in the middle of the reception area. There was no one else there, but I sensed that I wasn't being taken seriously. I had no intention of unpacking the envelope there.

"Is there somewhere private we could go?" I said, eyeing the PC.

DI Wren sighed and turned to a door behind him, punching a number into a pad. The door opened and he led me through into a long narrow corridor.

"Hang on," he said, "I'll just see if there's a free room."

I stood still as he walked away, disappearing through a door at the far end. A couple of officers came out of a room and passed me by and I moved back against the wall so as not to block things up. I was beginning to think

I'd been abandoned when the door at the far end of the corridor opened again and DI Wren came back, followed by someone else. The man behind him was talking to him, his voice deep and loud, like a deputy head teacher.

"Interview Room 1A," DI Wren said, stopping and giving me the briefest of smiles.

He turned and opened a door and that was when I got a look at the man behind him. He was taller and thinner and had a jacket and tie on. His jacket was buttoned up, his identity tag tucked in his top pocket. I knew this man, I was sure, but I couldn't think where from.

I sat down at a small table in the room. I began to unzip my rucksack and I felt the corner of the envelope.

"This is DI Brennan," he said, pointing at the other man. "You said it was something to do with Tyler Harrington?"

DI Brennan wasn't really looking at me. He had a Blackberry in his hand and he was scrolling down reading something. It gave me a few uninterrupted seconds to look at his face.

I did know him. I shifted about in my seat.

"Well? What did you want to say, miss?"

"I. . ."

DI Brennan looked up from his Blackberry. His eyes seemed to catch mine.

"What's up, dear? Something to do with Tyler Harrington?" he said, his voice strong.

He was the man in the photographs on Tyler's memory stick. The younger man in the car who had been grinning alongside the man I thought was Marty Robertson. For a minute I couldn't speak. My mouth was open and my tongue felt dry. The photograph had shown a police officer talking to Marty Robertson with Billy Rob waiting on the pavement. Something inside me deflated. I'd come for help and found myself in a worse mess.

"I wanted to come and see you. . ."

They both looked at me. DI Brennan slipped his Blackberry into a side pocket.

"I came here because. . ."

I realized that I still had my fingers on the corner of the envelope. I pushed it down and zipped the rucksack up.

"I came because I've been worried about Tyler. He seems to have gone missing."

"We've not got a report of a missing person, miss," DI Wren said.

I wanted to get up and leave but couldn't. I continued talking.

"He left hospital and no one seems to know where he is."

"Are you a relative?" DI Brennan said in a brisk way.

"I'm his friend."

"It's up to his family to report him missing," DI Brennan said, perching himself on the edge of the table so that he was closer to me than the other officer.

"I know, but I've been worried about him."

"Are you his girlfriend?" DI Brennan said.

"No, I'm just a friend."

DI Brennan stood up and began patting his pockets. He pulled out a mobile phone and began pressing buttons.

"Are you going to take this seriously?" I said, irked.

I decided that I didn't like this man.

"Well, miss, Tyler's *friend* or *girlfriend*, whatever you are," DI Brennan said. "Tyler and I are old friends. I know him pretty well and I wouldn't waste any time worrying about him. You're not even the first girl who's come looking for him today, isn't that right, Mike? I think he's probably shacked up with some new love that you don't know about. That's the way of the world, I'm afraid."

I must have had a shocked look on my face.

"Now, Norman. No need to upset the girl," DI Wren said.

DI Brennan made a *tsk*ing sound and left the room. The door slapped shut behind him.

"I'm sorry to have bothered you," I said, standing up.

"Don't worry about him. Norman's got a lot on his mind. The truth is we do only deal with missing persons through parents and next-of-kin," DI Wren said, softly.

The words *next-of-kin* hung in the air in a foreboding way.

I moved to the door. I edged sideways past the police officer, who became very talkative then and asked me which school I went to and what exams I was taking. I gave short replies all the way up the corridor and was relieved when I was on the other side of the door back in the reception area. Looking round, I saw that the WPC had gone from the counter and had been replaced by a grey-haired man in uniform who was talking to someone on the telephone.

I found I was trembling. In the interview room I'd

stayed calm and had to think quickly, but now that I was on my own, I felt this rising panic.

Out on the street I stood for a moment wondering what to do. I couldn't give Tyler's envelope to the police now and I had no idea what I was going to do with it. I walked to the bus stop, trying to think. I leaned back on the bus shelter and gazed at the traffic going by. I pictured DI Norman Brennan, who had been in the photographs. Tyler had saved those images and hidden them away so they had to *mean* something. Was it possible that Norman Brennan had been working undercover? Had he been collecting evidence about Marty and Billy Robertson's involvement in drugs? Or was he a crooked policeman, involved in Marty Robertson's shady world?

"Excuse me," a voice said.

I turned round. It was the girl who had been in the police station when I was there.

"Yes?"

"I couldn't help overhearing you asking about Tyler."

I nodded, not sure what to expect.

"I was in the station? I was trying to find out what's happened to him?"

That was what DI Wren meant when he said, *I thought you said there were two girls*. She was the other girl who had been asking about Tyler.

She was smiling and standing very close to me. She was taller than me and her hair was pulled back in some kind of clip. Her skin was the colour of dark wood. She had studs in her ears, bright red, the same colour as her top.

She was wearing a lot of perfume but I could also smell a faint tang of tobacco.

"Who are you?" I said. "How come you left the police station without speaking to a detective about Tyler?"

"I'm Flo. Short for Florence. Tyler's friend? I haven't seen him for a while. I was waiting for ages in there and when you came in I thought it might confuse the police to have two girls asking about him, so I came out. Did they tell you anything?"

I shook my head. This was the girl I had seen Tyler with a couple of times in recent months. Tyler's *girlfriend*, I had thought.

"I haven't seen him for a while," she went on. "I've been away this last week and when I got back I found a voicemail on an old mobile of mine. I hadn't realized that it was from him. It was sent from a number I didn't recognize so I didn't take much notice of it. It was only yesterday I listened to it. That was when I heard he was in hospital. I rang him but there was no answer. I rang the hospital, but by then he wasn't there any more."

"He left yesterday."

"Do you know where he is?"

I shook my head.

She was silent for a minute. She looked around the street. She seemed to be thinking about something.

"Are you off somewhere now?" she said.

"I'm going to school. To sixth form. . ."

"I'll give you a lift. We can talk in my car. Look, it's just over there. That Mini, see?"

She pointed to a silver car. It was parked tightly in between two vans. It was exactly the same as the one I had been staring at the previous evening when I was in the café with Jimmy Connelly.

"It'll be good to talk to someone about Tyler. I'm going out of my head with worry! Come on. . ."

She put her hand lightly on my elbow and steered me towards the car. She kept talking all the time about how she hadn't seen Tyler for a while, how she'd been busy at work, how she'd had to go to conferences and training and on top of that her mum wasn't well. Her conversation was like a rushing stream and her words carried me along until I was at the passenger door.

I found myself opening it and getting into her car.

FOURTEEN

Florence drove slowly, her gears crashing from time to time.

"I'm Ashley Littlewood," I said. "I'm a friend of Tyler's cousin Beth."

"You must be close. To go to the police about him."

"Just a friend," I said. "Are you his girlfriend?"

Florence laughed. "No, I'm his mate. I met him last summer. My boyfriend was a courier and he worked with Tyler sometimes. We hung around for a bit."

"Right. You know that he got beaten up?"

"He said in the phone message."

"I saw him in the hospital. He looked terrible."

"Did he?"

I nodded.

"Did he say anything to you? About who attacked him?"

I shook my head.

Florence's nails had caught my attention. They were blood red, filed in perfect half moons. They matched her top and her studs. She sighed suddenly. She stretched out her hand and with one rounded nail pushed the off button on the radio. The car went quiet, the music stopping. I hadn't noticed the music at all until it went off.

"Ashley, you're a bit of a surprise to me. I thought I knew all of Tyler's friends but I don't remember him talking about you."

"We weren't that close. . . We were once, but lately, well, for a long time really. . ."

I began to try and explain and then I thought, *Why do I have to tell this girl about me and Tyler?*

"You know what?" I said. "I'm a friend of his. You'll have to take my word for it."

She nodded. She drove on quietly for a couple of moments, staring out of the windscreen, her eyes flicking up to the rear-view mirror from time to time.

"I'll be honest with you, Ashley. I'm really worried about Tyler. I don't know how well you knew him but he was in with a lot of bad people."

"Marty Robertson and Billy Rob."

"They are dangerous."

"I know he sold drugs for them."

"Did you know he was trying to get away from it? He wanted to give it up."

I shook my head.

"He's supposed to be starting this computer course in January. He's had it fixed up for a while. He was going to move on. Leave all this stuff behind him."

That was a surprise. I had got used to the fact that Tyler had chosen the road he wanted to go down. Even though Jimmy had told me the true circumstances of that decision, I still pictured Tyler working in the shadows. I saw him in a hoodie, reaching out to a passing car, giving over a small packet or plastic bag and taking a folded up twenty-pound note in return. I never once imagined him walking to college with a rucksack full of files and plastic wallets and highlighters.

"If you're Tyler's mate, how come you haven't seen him for a while?"

"I've been busy. We just drifted apart."

"But he contacted you."

"On Monday. He made the call late on Monday night."

Monday was the day before I visited him. "What did he sound like?"

"You know what? He was troubled. Actually he was in a state."

Something occurred to me. Had he rung Florence to ask her to go and get the envelope? This thought gave me a twinge. Had I been second on his list?

"You all right? You look like you're about to burst into tears," Florence said.

"I'm just worried about him." Then I remembered that Jimmy had first come to me on Monday *afternoon*. If I had agreed to go, would he have rung Florence at all?

"You're not some new girlfriend, are you? Don't tell me that Tyler has fallen in love!"

I shook my head.

"Sorry," she said, "I shouldn't be joking at a time like this."

We were getting close to my school.

"It's the next turn on the right," I said.

"Did Tyler ask you to look after something for him," she

suddenly said, her voice different, harder, "when you went to visit him in hospital?"

The question threw me. I didn't know how to answer. A bus pulled out from a stop, though, cutting right across the path of the Mini, and Florence hooted the horn and slammed on the brake. I gave a weak smile and tugged at my seat belt to make sure it was fastened.

"They employ old-age pensioners to drive buses now!" she said.

I was still working out what to say. Tyler had told me to tell no one. Today I'd already tried to tell the police and now Florence was asking. This girl who until fifteen minutes ago I had never met.

She manoeuvred the car into the inside lane, just avoiding a cyclist who was coming up. She made a *tsk* sound and then fiddled about in the door compartment, pulling out a bag of sweets. She took one out and spent a few moments undoing the wrapper with her teeth and one hand, then passed the bag across to me. I let it lie on my lap. All the while I was thinking of the envelope sitting innocently in my bag. What if I gave it to her? Maybe that was why Tyler rang her on Monday evening. I had refused to go and see him and he needed someone to pick up the envelope. That meant that he *trusted* her. If I gave it to her, it would be out of my hands. She could decide what to do with it.

"What was I saying?" she said as we got nearer to my school.

"You asked me if Tyler gave me something to look after."

"Did he?"

But I didn't want to give it over. Whatever the situation was with the phone call or who was first and who was second choice, the fact was that I had it and it was *my* responsibility to look after it until Tyler told me differently. I'd already tried to give it to the police and that might have been a disaster.

"No," I said, "he didn't give me anything."

There was an uncomfortable silence. I took a sweet out of the bag and concentrated on opening it, twisting the cellophane until it slid out, then popping it into my mouth. I had the envelope. I had to take care of it.

"Here we are," I said, pointing to a parking space. "You can drop me off here."

"You're sure Tyler didn't ask you to hold *something* for him, or *do* anything for him?" Florence said, as the car slowed down.

"No," I said.

I put the bag of sweets on the dashboard and pushed the door open seconds before we came to a complete stop. I struggled out of my seat, pulling my rucksack by its fastener.

"Hang on a minute," Florence said, opening the glove compartment.

I stood awkwardly until she pulled out a card and handed it to me.

"My mobile number's on that, email too; just in case you want to chat."

She was holding it in mid-air. I had to take it, otherwise

it would have looked downright rude. I closed the door and in a second the Mini moved away from the pavement and off up the road.

The card was mint green and had silver lettering on it.

Florence Monk
Manicurist

I put it into my bag and walked off in the direction of school.

FIFTEEN

I found Beth in the common room. She was reading a magazine and seemed pleased to see me, but I sensed wariness, as if underneath she was a tiny bit angry. There were a few other kids about, mostly in pairs huddled together in soft chairs because it was cold. The sixth-form common room doors kept swinging open, allowing chilly blasts to career into the room as kids came in and out. Outside it was break and the younger years were running round the playground.

"What's going on, Ashe, with you and Tyler?" she said as soon as I sat down.

I told her about my visit to the hospital a couple of days before. Then I talked about the previous Christmas and about my continuing feelings for Tyler. The rest, what he did for Dan, the envelope and its contents, I kept to myself. It wasn't that I didn't trust Beth, but I didn't want to put her in the position of knowing something about someone in her family and having to keep it a secret.

"I still have feelings for Tyler," I said. "I've always had strong feelings for him but I kind of pushed them down. He's your cousin and I knew you wouldn't approve; that's probably why I didn't tell you."

"It was a year ago, though. Surely you've got over him by now?"

I didn't know how to answer her. It was a strange phrase, *Got over him*. It didn't describe my feelings at all. I got over my relationship with Tyler the night I saw him selling drugs, but I never *lost* my feelings for him. They just lay there somewhere deep inside so that I almost forgot I had any feelings for him at all. Then I would see him, like I had the previous Friday, and my emotions would flood out.

"I thought I had," I said, my hands flapping about as I was speaking, "and now he's hurt and on top of that he's missing. . ."

"But we don't know that he's actually *missing*," Beth said, putting her hand on my arm and squeezing it. "We just know that he's left the hospital."

"But if you'd seen him in the hospital. . . He was weak as water. He had stitches in his head, his ribs were bandaged up, he couldn't walk. His mum and dad must have seen him like that."

"They did. My aunt is really upset."

"But they haven't reported him missing?"

I thought of DI Wren's comments, *We only deal with missing persons through parents or next-of-kin.*

"My mum says they never know where he is. He lived with Jimmy Connelly until about a month ago. He moved out and didn't tell them. He just does what he wants."

He didn't live with Jimmy any more. Jimmy hadn't said a word about that when I'd seen him the previous evening.

"But what if, this time, he's been taken away? What if he's in actual danger?"

"Wouldn't he have cried out? Why would he let someone push him out of hospital in a wheelchair if he thought they were going to hurt him? In broad daylight? In the middle of hundreds of people who work there?"

I was bursting with frustration.

He told me he was in trouble. He asked me to look after something for him. He has pictures of a local drug dealer talking to a policeman. I don't know whether to trust that policeman or not. Tyler's frightened. Something is very wrong.

"He will turn up. Three weeks he was missing last summer. Honestly, my aunt thought he was dead."

"I know," I said, defeated.

"Come round my house tonight. My mum and dad are going out and I'm babysitting. I can cook a meal. You could bring Dan?"

"I'm not in the mood," I said. "Why don't you ask Dan? I'm sure he'd like to come."

"You think so?"

"Sure."

After school I walked Beth to her bus stop. I was quiet and she kept asking me if I was all right. I must have looked a little tearful because she pulled a crisp, folded cotton hanky from her bag. One corner of it was lace. She pushed it at me and gave me a hug.

"It'll be all right," she said. "Tyler will turn up and then maybe you can sort out your feelings for him."

"Thanks," I said, crumpling the hanky up in my hand.

I watched her get on the bus and stood still until it had driven away. I walked home. When I got there the house was empty. I went up to my room and took Tyler's envelope out of my rucksack and put it back into my wardrobe. I covered it up with clothes, then I sat down at my desk.

What was I going to do?

Tyler must be somewhere. But where?

Thirty minutes later I walked out of Mile End station. Further up, across the road, I could see the purple neon sign that flashed on and off: *Foneswapshop.com*, Marty Robertson's business. I walked towards it. I'd seen the shop a number of times when I was passing on a bus or in a car. After things ended with Tyler I always viewed the shop with some trepidation, as though I expected him to walk out of it at any minute.

Now I didn't expect to see him at all.

So why was I heading there? I wanted to have a look at Marty Robertson or Billy Rob close up; to see inside the shop; to look at their business. Maybe I also wanted to be in the place where Tyler had worked. Anything was better than sitting in my bedroom glancing regularly at the shelf in my wardrobe where the envelope was.

I was tense as I walked towards the shop.

A sign spanned the window front, which was floor to ceiling glass, and through it I could see a brightly lit up shop with soft chairs and a wall of mobile phone displays. *We Can Get Any Phone in 24 Hours*, a sign across the counter announced. On the wall at the back of the shop was a small television screen that was showing some action movie. A man was sitting behind the counter staring at it. I felt a pang of disappointment. There was no sign of Marty Robertson or Billy Rob.

I walked into the shop anyway and stood with my back to the counter, looking at the rows of phones that were all mounted on the wall. My eye travelled up and down just to give the impression that I was interested in buying one. I found an expensive model.

"Could I swap my phone in for this?" I said, loudly, pointing to the super-slim touch phone in the centre of all the others.

The man dragged his eye away from the television screen. He looked at me with suspicion, as if he knew I didn't have the funds and wasn't a serious shopper.

"It's my birthday soon and my dad's going to give me some money."

He seemed to sigh, as if he still didn't believe me. He pointed a remote at the screen and the volume went down.

"What you got now?" he said, lazily.

As I pulled my phone out of my pocket I heard noises from above, creaking as though someone was walking across a floor. The man looked up as well and seemed to visibly stiffen, sitting upright on his chair. After a moment he took my phone from me and was mildly impressed.

"Not bad," he said. "Pretty new, I'd say. What do you want to upgrade it for?"

"Oh, you know. My mate's got a better phone," I said, in a silly girly voice.

He started to flick through some papers in front of him. "I'm not sure what kind of deal we could do," he said. "I'd have to speak to the boss. . ."

A part of the wall opened up at the back of the shop. I was surprised. I hadn't noticed a door there. A man in a leather jacket came out holding a number of boxes, which he placed on the counter. He had a satchel bag across his front, which made him look a bit like a schoolboy. The door behind him hung open as he stacked the boxes sideways like dominoes and then counted them.

Then Billy Rob came out of the doorway.

I recognized him immediately. I'd seen him in the The Cheese and Ale a year before and I'd had glimpses of him from time to time in pubs and gigs. I'd also seen him in the photos on Tyler's memory stick.

"The Camden address first, then Wimbledon," he said.

"I think the Metropolitan Line's OK now, so Great Portland Street will do for the Euston address," the man with the leather jacket said.

Billy Rob nodded. I felt a twinge of anguish. This was what Tyler had done for Marty Robertson. Delivering phones all over London.

"I'm off," the man said, picking the boxes up and putting them into his bag. He pulled a woolly hat out of his pocket and went out of the shop.

"Are you serving this young lady, Phil?" Billy Rob said, looking me up and down.

"Yep! She's interested in an upgrade and we're just talking through her options."

Billy Rob walked past me without a word. He stood with his back to me, staring through the shop window at the road outside.

"I heard these phones were good as well," I said, pointing to a picture on the front of a catalogue that was on the counter. "Do the apps come as part of the package?"

"Possibly," Phil said, looking unsure.

"What about a contract?" I said. "Would it be cheaper to get the handset with a contract?"

"It would," Phil said, on firmer ground, "and we can arrange that, but we can also do pay as you go. Your dad might prefer that. You know what you teens are like with your talking on the phone!"

"Um. . ."

"Phil, you got the flyers and business cards that Dad asked for?" Billy Rob said without turning round.

"In a box out back. Shall I put them on display?" Phil said.

No answer came.

"Why don't you grab a chair and have a look at this catalogue," Phil said, pushing a couple of glossy catalogues at me. "There's usually FAQs at the back, so that will answer your questions. I can work out a price when you've made up your mind."

I pulled the catalogues together and carried them across to one of the soft chairs. I sat down facing Billy Rob's back. One of his feet was tapping rapidly but the rest of him was completely still. Outside, beyond the shop window, the traffic edged forward. Many vehicles had their lights on even though it wasn't quite dark. From behind me I could hear the sound of things being moved around. I flicked through the pages of the phone catalogue, staring intently at pictures of phone after phone.

Phil's voice came through the door, breathless.

"Here we are. I'll just put them here."

He put a small box on the counter and was taking a slim pile of business cards out of it and some glossy leaflets. Then he handed one of them to Billy Rob, looking round at me briefly. I gave him an encouraging smile and then went back to flicking through the pages.

"What about that other thing? That troublesome package? That all sorted out?" Billy Rob said, lowly.

I stopped turning the pages. I listened hard. Phil's voice seemed to drop down to his boots.

"Marty took it south of the river," he said. "I think it's quietened down a bit."

"Can't let these packages get too full of themselves."

"No."

"What if the package makes trouble?"

I felt my throat go dry. I listened as hard as I could but I missed a bit of Billy's reply.

". . .might have to have another swim. Quite close to the water, after all." Phil laughed out loud.

"Here's the old man," Billy Rob said, his voice normal now.

I looked out of the window as a car pulled up outside

120

the shop. It parked half up on the pavement. I got up. Phil turned round and looked mildly surprised, as if he'd forgotten I was there. I put the catalogues back on the counter. I saw the leaflets and cards that Phil had brought out.

"Shall I take one of these to show my dad?" I said.

"Sure, take what you want," he said.

I took a leaflet that said *foneswapshop.com*. I also picked up a couple of the business cards. Phil and Billy Rob had walked out of the shop and I followed them.

"I'll tell my dad about your phones," I called.

Phil nodded but he'd lost interest in me. Billy Rob didn't look round. They were both standing to attention at the car. In the driver's seat was an older man in sturdy black glasses. It was Marty Robertson, the man in the photographs. I walked off towards the underground station. I looked back a couple of times but they had gone into the shop.

On the tube I got a seat. Once I was sitting down I seemed to deflate, my shoulders sloping, my arms across my chest, concave. If I had had somewhere to rest my head I might have closed my eyes. Instead I stared between the people opposite at the windows and the dark tunnel that appeared to be speeding past us.

That troublesome package.

They had been talking about Tyler, I was sure. Or was I just reading too much into it? Whatever it was, Marty had taken it *south of the river*.

I thought back over the whole day. I'd met DI Brennan and I'd got close to Billy Rob. I'd also hooked up with

Florence. I fiddled with the pocket on my rucksack and pulled out her card. *Florence Monk, Manicurist.* Something didn't feel quite right about Florence. Her nails had been spectacularly nice, but she didn't seem like a *Manicurist.*

I was no closer to finding out where Tyler was.

Was Marty Robinson holding him somewhere, south of the river? To punish him for something? *Can't let these packages get too full of themselves.* And what was it they had said? *Might have to have another swim.* Tyler had already been in the canal once.

I took the other business cards out of my pocket. They were for two different companies. Bizzphones and Ezeecalls. They both had email addresses and phone numbers to contact. Each of them had the words *Value For Money* across the bottom. Did these companies also belong to Marty Robertson? Did they have offices south of the river?

The tube pulled into the Bethnal Green station and I got out as a bunch of younger schoolkids from my school pushed past me to get on.

"Hey!" I called out angrily.

A couple of them swore at me, but the others just broke into laughter. I stood on the platform fuming as the doors closed over. I felt like kicking something.

Was Tyler's life in danger? I remembered what my brother had said a year ago about the boy who had got killed by a hit and run driver. Then the newspaper article came into my mind, the one in Tyler's envelope. TEENAGER STABBED IN PARK ATTACK.

Six days ago Tyler had been left for dead in the canal.

Three teenage boys.

Now Tyler had disappeared.

What was I going to do? I was girl of seventeen, not a police officer or a private detective. This wasn't a made for TV drama, *plucky young teen thwarts drugs villain and saves boyfriend.* This was me; Ashley Littlewood, A level student, friend of Beth, sister of Dan, loving daughter, ex-girlfriend of Tyler Harrington. What could I do?

This was the question I asked myself all the way home.

SIXTEEN

I woke up the next day with a sense of determination. It was Friday. Almost a week since I'd heard about the attack on Tyler. The previous night, as I was trying to go to sleep, I'd thought about going to Tyler's parents and telling them everything. The trouble was I still wasn't sure of what was going on. What if I went to them and told them things that Tyler didn't want them to know? Or stuff that might get him into further trouble with the police? He'd already been in prison once. What if I was wrong and he really had just gone off on his own?

Until I knew the whole story I didn't want to tell anyone.

But what if Tyler *was* being held somewhere, against his will? What if he was being threatened or hurt? I remembered Billy Rob's phrase, *the troublesome package*. Was I reading too much into that?

I didn't have a class until the afternoon and I decided to *do* something. I turned my laptop on. Dan came in while I was waiting for it to load up.

"How do you find the address of a company?" I said.

"What is it? A shop? You can just put it in Google," he said. "What's it for?"

"Some research project. Key Skills stuff."

"You could go on the Companies House website. Every company should be registered there with an address."

"Thanks," I said, turning back to the computer.

"Don't forget to save it," he said.

"What?" I was tapping the keys, pressing *search*.

"On the memory stick. Remember?"

"Oh yeah," I said, looking round, my eye catching my bunch of keys on the desk. I'd completely forgotten about the gold memory stick that he had bought for me.

"Went round Beth's last night."

"I know."

"She's nice."

"You have known her for years. It's not like you've just met her."

"I know that. But she seems different now. Or maybe I'm different."

He walked out of my room and I thought, *Yes, you are different. In a good way, and it cost Tyler a lot.* It was probably something that Dan would never know.

I went on the Companies House website and put *Foneswapshop* into the search engine. A list came up and I clicked on a number that was next to the company name. The details came up in a second. The company address: *1187 Mile End Road*. It was the shop that I'd visited the day before. On my desk were the two business cards I'd picked up. I put the first company name, Bizzphones, into the search engine. I clicked on the company number and the same address came up. I picked up the other card,

Ezeecalls, and did the same. This time a different address came up.

Ezeecalls, 2 Bryan Street, Rotherhithe, SE16, UK

Rotherhithe was on the *south* side of the River Thames.

The word *Bryan* stood out. Bryan was on the label of the keys in Tyler's envelope. I'd thought it was a person's name but it was a street name. I was instantly excited. I went on Google Maps and put the postcode into the search engine. It was close to the river, about ten minutes' walk from Canada Water tube.

A beep sounded. It was a text from Beth.

No word about Tyler. See you this aft. Love Beth XXX

I was instantly touched. Beth and I didn't usually put endearments in our texts or emails, but she knew that I was upset. I got up, collected my travel card, my map and my keys and left the house.

Canada Water was one of the new stations on the Docklands Light Railway. I walked to Bow Church station and sat in the front of the driverless train as it wove its way through East London. The DLR trains were small, just three or four carriages, and they seemed to snake through estates and factories and bits of scrubland. The twists and turns and the lack of a driver meant that it often felt a bit like a pleasure park ride. Outside, the day was grey with dark puffy clouds. It wasn't as cold as it had been but the sky looked heavy with rain. Up ahead was the skyline of Canary Wharf. It was half-a-dozen skyscrapers which stood together like some futuristic castle in the distance. Around it was the flat lands of Docklands. Once it had been completely deserted with closed factories and desolate warehouses. Now it was stacking up with apartment blocks. New ones appeared every week, as if they had been built with Lego.

Out the other side of the train I could see the giant structures of the Olympic Park. Rows of cranes sat around the main stadium like delicate birds peeping over the top.

I sat back and let the scenery pass me by.

I changed lines at Canary Wharf and soon arrived at Canada Water. I took out my map and looked at it. I headed out from the station, turning the map sideways so that I could work out which way to go. The streets were empty apart from a couple of mums with pushchairs. It was past ten. Kids would be in school and most people would be at work. There was traffic but it was flowing freely. A white van raced past me towards the river. On the back it had a West Ham sticker. I waited for a bus to pass and then I crossed the road.

In a few moments I was on the corner of Bryan Street.

I looked along it. It was a narrow street with cars parked on either side and just enough space for one car to drive down the middle. On each side of the street were high buildings, three or four storeys. I could tell by the Juliet balconies that some were apartment blocks. Others were just flat fronted with vertical blinds slicing up the windows: offices, I thought.

The address I had was *2 Bryan Street*. The buildings in front of me were numbered in the fifties so I was at the wrong end. I walked down the side with the odd numbers, looking ahead for the other end of the street. The buildings became shabbier as I went along. In one place there was a complete gap between two of them and a fence erected along the front. Looking up at the adjacent wall, I could see soot and the burned remains of timbers. The pavement was rucked as well. There were for-sale signs and one building had a sign for an auction in a couple of weeks' time. As I got towards the end of the road I slowed down and looked over the parked cars at the end building. Number two.

It was three storeys and stood back off the road slightly. A sign had been erected by it. Waterside Apartments Exciting Development. Underneath was a line drawing of a block of apartments with bushy trees on each side. It was 2 Bryan Street. The building was shabby but its brickwork had been painted white at some point. In contrast, the wooden entrance door looked brand new. The ground-floor windows had metal shutters drawn across them. The windows on the floors above were not shuttered but had been roughly whitewashed, the streaks from the paint still visible. It gave the whole building an ethereal look, like something in a ghost story. To the side of the front door was a metal post box. That also appeared to be brand new. I looked around and made sure no one was on the street then I walked across the road and saw a tiny sign on the post box that said Ezeecalls Ltd.

The big wooden door was solid. There was a Yale lock in the middle. In the top right-hand corner was a Chubb lock. Halfway down the bottom of the door was another Chubb lock.

Three locks for three keys. The set in Tyler's envelope looked brassy and shiny as if they'd never been used.

I walked backwards across the street and looked intently up at one of the windows. I wondered if Tyler might be up there. I half thought of picking up a stone and throwing it, but it was a stupid idea because if he was there he would be locked away or restrained. He might even have one of Marty Robertson's people with him. I would only be drawing attention to myself. I stood for a few moments staring at the building, wondering what to do.

"What you doing?" a voice said.

I spun round. Billy Rob was walking towards me. He was holding a chunky set of car keys, jiggling them. I took a step back away from him, my face in a frown. I looked up and down the street, wondering where he had sprung from.

"Nothing," I said. "I'm not doing anything."

"Why are you looking up there? What you looking for?"

"I'm not," I said, "I'm just meeting a friend."

"What? Here?"

"She works in an office."

I pointed further up the street.

"So what you looking up there for?" he demanded, stepping closer.

"Hey! You don't own the pavement. I can wait wherever I want," I said.

"Don't I know you? Weren't you in my shop yesterday?"

"What shop?" I said, rolling my eyes exaggeratedly. "Look, get lost. I'll wait for my friend up the road."

I shrugged and walked off, looking down at the ground, taking long steps to get away from Billy Rob. I was tensing my shoulders, half expecting him to walk after me and grab me by the coat. I was angry, tutting to myself. The pavement was cracked up in places and I stepped carefully. Why I hadn't I kept an eye out for a car pulling up? Why hadn't I been more careful? Why had I let myself get caught there? I passed the burned-out building and let my shoulders relax a little, thinking that I'd left him behind, when I heard the sound of a car coming.

I did not want to face Billy Rob again. I stepped sideways and walked close up to the edge of the buildings and heard the car come closer. I would not run. I would keep calm. I looked down at the paving stones flashing past. I made myself put one foot after another. The car had slowed and was alongside me. I could feel it there: the hum of its engine, the muffled sound of a radio from inside, the splutter of its exhaust. The corner was twenty paces away. If I could just walk fast enough to get out of the street then there might be other people around.

A beeping sounded. It was insistent. I had to look round.

It was the silver Mini. Florence Monk was driving. I looked back down the street. There was no sign of Billy Rob. Florence had lowered the passenger window and was leaning across the car.

"Get in. You and me need to talk. Serious talk," she called.

I stood for a minute, uncertain.

"Come on!" she shouted, pushing the passenger door open.

I got in and she drove off without a word.

SEVENTEEN

Florence parked her car in a supermarket car park and walked ahead of me into the café area. She was still wearing the high heels she'd had on the previous day in the police station. On top of these she had skinny jeans and a parka. Her hair was covered with a crocheted yellow beret. She was carrying a huge handbag with chains and baubles hanging from the handles. As she moved they made chinking noises that sounded like wind chimes.

She was walking in a clipped fashion, as though she was annoyed with me. It reminded me of a head of year leading a troublesome student from the classroom to her office. I wondered if she was going to give me a telling-off.

"Tea? Coffee?" she said.

"Fizzy water."

I chose a table as she went to the counter.

The café was half empty. There were a couple of workmen tucking into late breakfasts and a mum with a baby in a high chair. I felt hot all of a sudden. The dash up Bryan Street had left me stressed. I scooped my keys out of my pocket and took my coat off, laying it on the chair next to me. I grabbed my keys and fiddled with the heart-shaped fob. My hands were shaky and I remembered my panic when I'd thought that Billy Rob was following me in his car. I let my fingers run along the serrations of my keys, dwarfed in number by the silly trinkets that I had attached to the key ring. I remembered then the big solid door to the house in Bryan Street. It had three locks, which matched the keys in Tyler's envelope.

"Here," a voice said.

A bottle of fizzy water sat on the table in front of me.

"Thanks," I said, opening it and talking a long gulp.

Florence's nails were painted yellow today. They stood out sharply against her mahogany skin. They were the shape of petals and then I noticed that her beret had a flower on the side. She obviously liked to be coordinated.

"Look, Ashley," she started, "there's some stuff I didn't tell you yesterday. . ."

I frowned. Looking straight at her, I realized then that she wasn't as young as I had taken her to be when I first saw her. She was in her early twenties or maybe even older. Her eye settled on my bunch of keys.

"What is this?" she said, smiling.

I shrugged. I didn't have to explain myself to her. I pushed the bunch to the side and drank some more water.

"What do you want?" I said.

"I didn't tell you everything about last summer. How come I got to be a mate of Tyler's," she said.

I sat back and folded my arms. There was something about her that I just didn't trust.

"My boyfriend, me and Tyler we used to hang around a lot together. Joe was a courier and he worked for Marty

Robertson. He and Tyler used to go for a drink after work and I'd meet up with them. I liked Tyler. He was a really good guy. He was funny. He made me laugh."

"Did they go drug dealing together?" I said.

Florence looked sheepish. "I know Tyler did quite a lot of stuff, but Joe just dabbled. I didn't like it. I didn't want him to but it was just a few quid here and there. It wasn't a *career*."

"Just a part-time job?"

"He didn't like doing it. He wanted to stop but it was hard to say no."

I was about to say something sarcastic but then I remembered my own brother Dan. Hadn't this all started with him not being able to say no?

"Anyway, that was how I knew Tyler."

I didn't know if she wanted me to say something. I kept quiet. I couldn't help wondering whether she was trying to make a friend out of me so that I would open up and tell her about Tyler's envelope.

"Then something happened to Joe. He got killed. Actually he got *murdered*."

I unfolded my arms. My cocky stance crumbled.

"He got stabbed late one night in a park. The police thought it was a race killing. They said that Joe was chased and attacked by a couple of white boys, but I don't think that's what happened. Tyler didn't think that that was what happened either."

"Joseph Lindsay," I said, softly.

"You know about Joe?" she said.

I thought of the clipping from the *Metro*, the headline, TEENAGER STABBED IN PARK ATTACK. It had been in Tyler's envelope and I hadn't known why it was there. Now I did.

"I'm sorry for you," I said.

She didn't say anything for a minute. Then she spoke.

"When Joe got stabbed, Tyler went a bit mad. He disappeared off for weeks. I thought, for a short time, that something had happened to *him*, but he'd just been abroad and when he came back he was calm. He told me he was sure that Billy Rob had something to do with Joe's death. He said that Marty Robertson had a contact in the police and that they were making it look as though Joe's death was a race killing."

The stuff in the envelope was beginning to make sense; the cutting and the pictures of Marty Robertson together with DI Brennan. It meant that the policeman was *not* working undercover. He was helping Marty Robertson in some way.

"Tyler stayed working for Marty and Billy because he wanted to find out what had happened to Joe."

A ringtone sounded. Florence reached down to her bag and rummaged in it. She pulled a mobile out and looked at the screen before answering it.

"I've just got to get this."

She stood up and walked away from the table towards the exit. I felt this rush of sympathy for her. Her boyfriend murdered. All her bright clothes and perfect nails now seemed like a camouflage. She looked uncomfortable on the phone. She wasn't doing much talking, just nodding a lot, as though someone on the other end of the line had loads to say. I kept thinking about DI Brennan. Had he been involved in a *murder*?

She'd left her bag open on the floor. A woman with a pushchair edged past it. One side of it had drooped and the contents were in danger of spilling out. I tweaked the rim so that it sat up. Inside, amid a load of junk, I could see three mobile phones. *Three*. Florence was talking on a phone over by the exit. That made four. Who owned four mobile phones?

She came back.

"Sorry. . ." She sat down again, pulling her bag up off the floor and putting it on to the table. She began to sort through it as if looking for something. I couldn't help but feel on edge.

"Sorry, I'm a bit distracted today. I'm just looking. . ."

She moved the bag and it hit my bottle of water and nudged my keys so that both of them were knocked off the table. The keys clattered on to the tiled floor and the bottle bounced and rolled away. I went after it. When I sat down again Florence was picking up my keys and replacing them on the table.

"I'm so clumsy. Sorry."

She put her bag on the floor again and looked a little peeved and flustered.

"Now, where were we?"

I instantly felt irked. It was the way she said *Where were we?* as if I was a job she was halfway through. Who was

Florence? She was so *convenient*: at the police station at the same moment I was there; in the street when I was looking at the white house.

"You were telling me about Joseph Lindsay."

"Look, Ashley. I need to get straight to the point here. I asked you yesterday if Tyler gave you something to look after. You said no."

I didn't answer so she went on.

"You remember I told you he rang me? Well I got two calls from him. The first one was on Monday night and he sounded awful, said he desperately needed to see me. The second call was on Tuesday night. In that call he sounded better, more together. He said he had important evidence against Marty and Billy. He said he'd left it with a trusted friend."

An uneasy feeling was growing in my chest. Florence hadn't told the whole truth the first time I met her. How could I be sure that she was telling the truth now?

"I think you were that friend, Ashley. If Tyler has given you something to look after then you should give it to me. You can trust me."

I didn't trust her.

"How do I know who you really are?" I said.

"I'm Tyler's friend. He hasn't got many friends at the moment, but I'm one of them."

I went quiet. Then I shook my head.

"Tyler didn't give me anything."

"I don't believe you," Florence said, lowering her voice. "Tyler found out what happened to Joe. He said he's got evidence. I think Marty Robertson knew Tyler had something on him. That's why he attacked him a week ago. Now he's disappeared and I'm certain that Marty Robertson has taken him. He'll want that evidence back. That's why you should give it to me. If he gets hold of whatever it is that Tyler's given you there'll be no reason to keep Tyler alive."

"You think they might *kill* him?"

I stared at her. Maybe *she* was working with Marty Robertson. Maybe it was her job to persuade me to give the envelope over.

"If you're so worried about Tyler why don't you go to the police?"

"Because I'm not sure how many policemen Marty Robertson might have on his payroll."

"So why did you go to the police station yesterday? You were there when I got there."

Florence looked uncomfortable.

"I was going to pretend that I was his girlfriend. I was just going to see if anyone would speak to me. When you turned up I thought you really were his girlfriend and that it would look odd if I was there claiming to be. . ."

She had an answer to everything. She had four phones in her bag. Who has four phones?

"I'm not saying anything," I said, getting up.

"OK," she said, tapping her yellow nails on the table. "You've got my mobile number. I think Marty Robertson will do Tyler some harm. You don't have to take my word for it. Look up the name Stuart Lister on the internet. See what articles you can find about him."

I turned to go but after a few steps she called my name. I swivelled round and saw her holding my keys in mid-air. I'd left them on the table. I snatched them off her and walked away. I didn't look back.

I didn't need to research Stuart Lister. He'd been killed in a hit and run early one morning. Billy Rob had used this fact to threaten my brother Dan and pressure him into selling drugs for him.

A year before. When it all started for Tyler.

EIGHTEEN

After leaving Florence Monk I strode towards the station. I got a tube and headed for home. I couldn't face school or Beth or anyone. Luckily my house was empty. I went up to my room and threw open the lid of my laptop. I waited for it to load up, then I typed the name Joseph Lindsay into Google. I clicked on the first listing, then the second, then the third. All of them gave the same story.

Joseph Lindsay was murdered in a park in West London. He was a long way from his home in Stratford. He died from three stab wounds, all to the chest. He was killed between midnight and two a.m. His body was discovered by a group of schoolchildren the following morning just before eight. They found him in a copse at the edge of Woodberry Park, Acton.

There were two different photos of Joseph.

Joseph Lindsay was a light-skinned black boy. He had dark eyes and his hair was cut very short. He had a wide smile and even teeth. It looked as though he had a stud in his nose but I couldn't be sure. In each picture he was wearing a white T-shirt. I wondered if he had been wearing one on the night he was chased and stabbed to death.

I closed my laptop down.

Just after two I went downstairs and made a sandwich, which I ate bite by bite without tasting. When I finished I was restless and didn't know what to do. I went back upstairs and got the envelope out of my wardrobe again.

I opened it, and the keys, the CD and the memory stick dropped out. The photocopy came next. I looked at it: *TEENAGER STABBED IN PARK ATTACK*. Joseph Lindsay, boyfriend of Florence, friend of Tyler. The date on it was July the seventeenth.

The newspaper said that it was a racist crime.

I picked up the CD and looked at it. Why was it in the envelope? How was it significant? I'd already checked that there was nothing hidden in the case. I opened it and took the glossy information leaflet out again. I flicked through the pages and held it up to the light in case there was something written on it. But there was nothing; it was just the lyrics of the songs and several pictures of members of the band. Then I looked at the CD itself.

There *was* something different about the disc. It wasn't a professionally produced CD. I hadn't noticed it the last time I looked. It had no words or designs on it. It was blank, silver, as if it was a download or a copy from someone else.

I went across to my laptop and slid the CD in and pressed the play button. In seconds I heard someone speaking; a recording of a conversation. Two men were talking to each other. The sound wasn't great but I could make out most of the words. I listened, straining my ears to catch everything that was said.

Who did you put in charge of the investigation?

One of my men. He's a good bloke. You can feel safe about him.

Will he want paying?

Everyone wants paying, Marty. You should know that.

What about the witnesses?

Someone I know. It's simple. She saw two white skinheads chasing Lindsay into the park. She's rock solid. She owes me.

And how much do I owe you?

Ten. That's what we agreed on.

You're expensive.

Bills to pay, Marty. We all have bills to pay.

Make the most of it. That should be the last problem I have for a while.

I expect there'll be someone else. It was the Lister boy last year, now Lindsay. You should choose your staff more carefully.

Then you'd be out of a job.

I've got a very good job and you know it. Protecting the public from drug dealers. . .

In the background were traffic noises, cars passing, horns beeping, a siren winging past.

I listened over again, pausing it from time to time.

One of the voices I'd heard before in the police station: DI Norman Brennan, the man in the photographs. I clicked on my files and opened up the photographs that I'd copied from Tyler's memory stick. I pressed *slide show* again and then I restarted the CD. It wasn't perfect. The words were out of sync with the pictures, but it was as if I were watching these two men speaking to each other.

Marty Robertson's voice got louder in places, as if he was moving back away from whatever it was that was recording the conversation.

It was the Lister boy last year, now Lindsey. You should choose your staff more carefully, DI Brennan said.

Florence and Tyler had been right. Marty Robertson had arranged the killing of these two boys and Tyler had found out about it and collected evidence. No wonder he had hidden this away. No wonder he had asked me to keep it safe.

I saved the recording on to a file on my laptop and removed the CD. Then I picked up the keys. Two Chubb keys and a Yale. They felt cold and new. The edges were sharp and a little jagged; they hadn't been worn away by frequent handling or constant use. I put them in my jeans pocket and put everything else back in the envelope. I placed it in my desk drawer, covering it with books.

I put my coat on and picked up my travel card.

Then I headed for Bethnal Green.

It was getting dark when I got out of the tube. *Second-Hand Furniture* was busy, the pavement lit up with light spilling from inside the shop. There was a couple outside, the man sitting on chairs and then standing up. The woman had a cigarette in her fingers and was touching the fabric of a lampshade on a yellowing standard lamp. Inside were a couple of youngish men pulling open the drawers of filing cabinets. Jimmy's dad was on the phone and Jimmy was standing by one of the men. He was wearing his puffa jacket as usual and I wondered if he ever took it off. When he saw me he frowned and said something to the two men and came out of the shop. His face was long, his body language unwelcoming. I didn't waste any time.

"I thought Tyler lived in your flat."

"He used to. He said it was too noisy. Moved out a couple of months ago."

"Where's he live now?"

"I don't know. What is this? The third degree?"

"Do you know Florence Monk?" I said. "She hung around with Tyler. Black girl."

He looked exasperated. Then he exhaled.

"Flo? Oh yeah, I know her. She picked Tyler up from the flat a few times. She was always round the pub. Haven't seen her in months, though."

He called her Flo. It sounded like an affectionate nickname. I wondered if that's what Tyler had called her. I couldn't think of her like that. To me she was Florence.

"Did you know Joseph Lindsay? Her boyfriend?"

"Joe was around a lot before. . ." His voice trailed off.

"He got stabbed."

Jimmy nodded. He looked across the road at a group of kids who were walking along. He seemed to square his shoulders at the sight of them. Then he turned back to me.

"Was Tyler upset about it?" I said.

"What do you think? He was Tyler's mate. They worked together. What is this?"

"I'm trying to help Tyler."

"Flo was upset about Joe; so was Tyler. Actually it was all Tyler ever talked about. Joe this, Joe that. . ."

"Florence says that Tyler has evidence that Joe was killed by Marty Robertson or Billy Rob."

"What?" Jimmy stiffened.

"Tyler thinks Joe's death wasn't a race crime, like they said in the paper."

"First I've heard of it. Tyler never said anything to me about it."

"That's what Florence says. What do you think?"

"Don't know. How should I know?"

"Jimmy, I need you to help me. I think I know where Tyler might be."

"Where?"

"At Marty Roberston's place in Rotherhithe? I think they might be keeping him there. I overheard them talking about a package. . ."

He shook his head, a look of impatience on his face.

"You think you know Tyler but you don't. You had a few weeks with him last year but that was it. He's not the person you knew. He disappears sometimes. That's what he's like. Last summer he went off for three weeks. No one knew what had happened to him. Then he turns up."

"But he was *taken* out of the hospital."

"How do you know he didn't make a call and ask someone to come and get him out of hospital?"

"I saw him the day before. He was in no fit state. He was scared."

"All the more reason for him to get out of hospital. If he was scared of Billy or Marty then it made sense for him to get out of sight, to fade away for a while."

I didn't answer. It was a good point. Inside, though, I felt that Tyler was in trouble. I couldn't explain it, I just *felt* it.

"Do you know where he is?" I said.

"No."

"Then, please, come with me."

He frowned.

"Come with me to Rotherhithe. When it's dark. We can have a look around. If there's no sign of anyone I can go inside the building. See if there's any clues."

"What are you, Sherlock Holmes?"

"I just need you to stand in the street and call me if anyone turns up."

"How you going to get in? Break down the door?"

I took the keys out of my jeans pocket and let them hang in the air between us. Jimmy looked at them, then back at me. I couldn't read his expression.

"Tyler gave them to me."

Jimmy shook his head, a look of ridicule on his face.

"Maybe Tyler's not there, but he gave me these keys and if they fit that door, then that place is significant."

"Why don't you just go to the police?"

"I can't go to the police because *they might be involved.*"

"Now the police are involved!" he said, rolling his eyes.

"Please. Will you help me?"

He shrugged. He nodded, slowly, unsurely.

"When can you get away?"

"An hour or so?" he said.

I nodded. "I'll wait in Chaplin's," I said.

He turned and walked back to the shop.

NINETEEN

Jimmy and I got the tube to Canada Water at about seven o'clock.

Jimmy hardly spoke. I was nervous so I ended up talking non-stop. I went over everything and then I started talking about the Olympics. I was just filling the empty minutes as we sped towards Rotherhithe. Outside the train, East London was like a giant building site. There was a moon in the sky which sat like a silver coin, heavy and bright. Jimmy didn't look out of the windows, he just stared down at his mobile. At one point I plucked his mobile from him and put my number on it. Then I forced him to take mine and tap in his number. We might need to contact each other, I said, and then went on talking about other times when I hadn't had someone's number and I'd needed it.

Eventually, when we pulled into Canada Water, I shut up.

I was so glad that I'd got Jimmy to come along. When we got out of the station and started to walk along the streets, he pulled a small torch out of his pocket and handed it to me. It wasn't something that I'd considered but it was a good thing to have and it made me feel better, as though Jimmy was a willing partner, not someone I had to drag along.

There were street lamps, but the buildings in the area were not well lit up. The apartment blocks seemed shadowy, and offices were either closed down for the day or were not being used at all. There were no corner shops to brighten up the gloom, and hardly any traffic passing through. In the distance I could see the Canary Wharf towers, all bright and twinkling, but around us, on the street in Rotherhithe, it was murky.

I led the way.

"It's down here," I said, "at the other end."

In daylight the street had been bright and clear, the line of the buildings visible. When I peered down the far end of the street, the buildings seemed to dwindle into darkness and I realized then that some of the street lights further down were not working.

"Come on, it's not far."

A short while later we were standing across the road from 2 Bryan Street. In the dark, the building looked even more ghostly. There were no lights on any of the floors. The new front door looked square and solid beside the crumbling brickwork and patched-up glass. Even the metal shutters looked strained and stretched, as if they belonged to different windows entirely. At the side the sign for the new apartment complex looked smart and businesslike. *Waterside Apartments Exciting Development*.

"You think Tyler's in there?" Jimmy said.

"I don't know."

We walked down the side of the building. The street there was narrow, more like a lane. There was a high brick wall for about twenty metres and then a wooden gate. I pushed against it but it was bolted. A small sign said *Protected by Riverside Security Ltd.* The brick wall continued to a corner. I backed across the street and looked up at the upper floors of the building. There was no sign of any light in any window.

The building was empty.

My confidence crumbled. Why would Tyler be there? The whole thing seemed ridiculous. What was I doing? I was grasping at straws, imagining myself as some kind of hero figure. Maybe Jimmy was right. Maybe Tyler had taken himself out of hospital and hidden himself *away* from Marty Robertson. He'd asked me to look after the envelope and now he was in a B and B in Kent or Essex somewhere, getting better, pulling himself back together, and here I was, hanging round the perimeter of an empty building thinking that I could save him.

Jimmy had walked back up the street towards the front of the building. I followed him, determined to call it off, to go back home. He turned the corner in front of me, so I quickened my steps, feeling uneasy about being in the dark in a deserted street that led down to the river. I got to the corner and heard a loud banging sound. Jimmy was knocking on the door of 2 Bryan Street with his fist. It was making a huge racket.

"What are you doing?" I said.

"Soon find out whether anyone's in or not," he said, stepping back, away from the door.

"No. . ."

"What? Changed your mind? Decided not to save Tyler after all?" he said, grinning at me.

Nothing moved inside. No lights went on; there was no sound of anyone coming down the stairs or along a hallway. I looked up the road. The other buildings seemed closed off and distant. They probably had triple glazing and wouldn't hear a bomb going off.

"I'm not sure. . ."

"Get your keys out, then," Jimmy said, smug.

"I'm not sure if this is a good idea."

"Come on. You said you were going to do it, so do it!"

I reluctantly got the keys out of my pocket. I *had* said I was going to do it. I stretched up and put one of the Chubbs in the top lock. It didn't move. I took it out, squatted down and tried it in the bottom lock. It turned. I felt my neck stiffen a bit with tension. I put the second Chubb in the top and unlocked it. Then I turned back to Jimmy.

"You should stand out of the way. If any cars stop or anyone walks along, ring me. You don't need to say a word, just let it ring twice and then stop. I'll know it's you."

"Will do," Jimmy said, jauntily.

He walked across the street and backed into the doorway of a building about ten metres away.

I fitted the Yale key into the lock. There was a soft click

and the door opened. Inside was just thick blackness. I stood for a second not knowing what to do. I took the torch out of my pocket and shone it. A small circle of light hung in the middle of the dark interior. I zigzagged the torch and saw a wide hallway with some stairs at the side. I put my hand inside and felt for a light switch. I found one and clicked it but no light came on.

I called out, "Tyler?"

I called again but there was no sound, no sign of life, nothing.

I looked round at Jimmy. He made a gesture with his hands for me to go on. I stepped inside the door. The building had three floors. I would have to look in every room and it meant going upstairs, in the dark. I felt a shiver of apprehension.

"What's the matter?"

Jimmy's voice came from behind me.

"I'm scared."

"Do you want me to come in?"

"No, you have to watch the street."

"Be quick then."

I took a deep breath and walked into the hallway and towards the first door. I found the handle and tried to open it. It was stiff and the door opened with a groaning creak. I shone the torch inside, swinging it round. It was a big room. There were a couple of filing cabinets against one wall but nothing else. I didn't linger; I walked on to the next door. It came open easily. I looked in. The room was much lighter, as though it was a different time of day there. I stepped inside. There was a window at the back which had diamond-shaped metal mesh across the glass. Moonlight shone through. The pattern of light spread across the floor, silver diamonds increasing in size like some bizarre board game. I found myself walking across oddly until I got to the back window. I saw the yard, big enough for lorries to park in. Beside the gate was a high stack of wooden pallets.

Something moved at the corner of my eye. I looked intently into the darkness. At first I thought it was a cat but it was moving differently: stiffly, slowly, nervously. It was a fox. I watched for a few moments as it stopped and sniffed at something on the ground. One of its paws moved as if to try and scrape or dig.

Then it looked up. I thought for a second it had seen me or smelled me close by but it was looking past me at the floor above.

A noise sounded that was coming from the ceiling.

A tap. Then another.

As if someone was tapping their foot on the floorboards above.

I looked up. I stood very still. Above me were long strip lights attached to the ceiling. I listened. Every part of me was stiff.

Tyler was up there. I *felt* it.

I walked across the room, still looking upwards, my heart swelling in my chest. I was *right*. I'd been right to come. He was here. I could feel it. I turned out of the room and went swiftly up the stairs. I didn't call out because my voice was stuck in my throat. I headed towards the back of the house, for the room above where I had been standing.

I didn't think. I didn't slow down.

I flung the door open and shone the torch around. I stopped when I saw something. I held my breath.

There, in the corner, sitting on a chair, was Tyler.

"Tyler!" I said in a half whisper.

I stepped forward, holding the torch on his face. His eyes were stony and there was something tight round his mouth. He looked dreadful, grim, as if I were the last person he wanted to see.

An awful feeling took hold of me. It flooded up through my legs and washed through my guts as the room light clicked on. I closed my eyes, blinded by the yellow glare. The room suddenly felt like it was full of people. I could hear them breathing, I could feel the heat from their bodies. I could *smell* them.

I opened my eyes, squinting in the bright light.

"Someone's come to get you, Tyler, my lad," a voice said. "Right on time as well!"

I took my hands away from my eyes. Billy Rob was standing there. He was smiling. It was fake and mocking. His eyes were sharp and cold.

He'd known I was coming.

TWENTY

This room had furniture in it. A desk and some chairs. There were a couple of filing cabinets against the wall that held a kettle and some glass jars for tea bags and coffee. On the desk were three mugs sitting companionably together. One of them had the word Hammers on it. The other two were white. There was a packet of HobNobs at the side, half eaten, the wrapping torn off in a spiral wilting on to the table.

A metre away Tyler was tied to a chair with a gag across his mouth.

I looked around in disbelief.

Standing beside Billy Rob was another man who I had never seen before. He had dark cropped hair and was wearing a hoodie and jogging trousers, as though he'd just come from the gym. He wasn't young, though. His hair was grey at the sides and at the corner of each eye were deep crow's feet. He walked across to where Tyler was and put one of his hands on Tyler's shoulder. It sat like a clamp and Tyler closed his eyes and looked down.

From behind I heard footsteps coming up the stairs. Moments later I saw Phil, the man from the phone shop. I expected him to be dragging Jimmy up the stairs but he was alone.

Where was Jimmy? Why hadn't he rung me as we'd planned?

"Well," Billy Rob said, looking at me, "we'll have to stop meeting like this."

I turned from one to the other. I had no idea what to say or do. I looked back at Tyler and saw, clearly now, that he couldn't move at all. It made me feel weak at the knees. All my thoughts of Tyler being held or imprisoned were from adventure stories. Escape was always possible: sliding down a rope, stealing a key, climbing out of a window. But Tyler looked ill, his skin pale and yellowish, shiny with sweat. The wound at the side of his eye was bloody, as if the stitches had burst. I looked away, down at his foot. The plaster cast was still there but now it was grubby and battered-looking, Tyler's toes sticking out, curling under.

I made a step to walk towards him but was stopped by a look from Billy Rob. He gestured to the other man.

"Take his gag off, Scot."

Scot pulled the gag roughly off and Tyler gasped for breath. His eyes met mine and then he closed them. He seemed ashamed. It made my throat burn looking at him.

"Let's get down to business," Billy Rob said.

For once Billy Rob wasn't wearing a suit. He had dark jeans on and a black zip-up jacket. The jeans had creases ironed into them, though, and the jacket looked as though it was brand new. His eye dropped down to the torch that I held in my hand.

"Ah!" he said. "That'll be mine. I told your young friend it would come in useful."

I held it out and he snatched it from me. *Jimmy.* My mind raced. He had given Jimmy the torch and Jimmy had given it to me. *Jimmy had been in on it.*

He was Tyler's friend. He had betrayed him.

"Now, miss. You have got something that I want."

I stared at Billy Rob.

"I'll make myself a bit clearer. Your friend Tyler here made a recording of a conversation between my dad and another man. I know this because he told me. He also took some photographs."

I looked back to Tyler.

"What he didn't tell me was who had possession of these things."

I winced. I was feeling faint. I was the only person standing straight up. I had nowhere to lean. The light in the room was unbearably bright; it seemed to be directly above me, pinning me to the spot.

"But I know that now and I'm willing to do a deal. I want the recording and photographs and I want them back tonight."

Billy Rob took a step towards me.

"If I get it I will let your friend Tyler go and I will say no more about it. Then we can go on living our lives as though this nasty little inconvenience hasn't happened."

I swallowed. I was too afraid to say anything.

"So, here's what we'll do. You go home and get the package."

I nodded.

"Oh! And take this with you."

He pulled a phone out of his pocket and held it out.

"Pay as you go. Not the sort of rubbish I usually carry round with me."

I took the mobile.

"I will call you at ten o'clock and tell you where to go. I'll have Tyler with me. You give me the package. I let him go."

I didn't answer.

"If you don't answer the phone or if I think you don't have the package then you won't see him again. Show her, Scot."

Scot squatted down behind the desk. He lifted up a pile of weights, the kind that were usually slotted on to dumb-bells. There were six or so, the size of saucers but thick and solid. He laid them on the surface of the desk. Then he picked up a couple of them in each hand.

"Demonstrate, Scot."

He put the weights in each pocket of his hoodie. There were four left on the desk.

"They go in the trouser pockets," Scot said, with a smile as though he were a salesman showing off some new product.

"My friend Tyler here will be wearing these weights and going for a swim," Billy Rob said. "We'll take him to the river. You won't see him after that. He'll be lying at bottom of the Thames for many years to come."

Tyler coughed and we all looked at him.

"Don't do it, Ashe," he whispered.

Scot's fist shot out and hit Tyler on the side of the head. He lurched to one side but the rope held him in his chair. His head seemed to hang loosely, as if he'd been knocked out. A wave of nausea rolled over me. I took a step towards him but Scot moved forward to block my way.

"It's time for you to go," Billy Rob said. "I'll ring you at ten on the dot."

I felt Phil's hand pulling at my arm and giving me a shove towards the door.

"One more thing," Billy Rob said, "I'm sure you've a got a computer? Everyone's got a computer these days. A desktop, laptop, notebook, iPad, Mac, whatever. You bring it with you when you come. I just need to check it over."

I nodded and he came towards me, his jovial manner gone, his face hard.

"Don't say a word to anyone about this. Don't mess me around. Not if you want to see him again."

"I won't."

I stumbled out of the room and down the stairs. Phil followed behind. He was humming lowly, as if this were an ordinary day and he was tidying up the shop. I pulled the big door open and stepped outside. The street looked misty. There was no sign of Jimmy. A second later the door slammed shut behind me and I heard the sound of bolts being pulled across it.

Then I started crying. And running.

TWENTY-ONE

As soon as I was out of Bryan Street I slowed down a bit. My breath was tearing across my chest and I was hiccuping out sobs. I wiped my nose with the back of my hand and put my head down and walked in the direction of the station. Every step I took I felt as if I were running away from Tyler. I pictured him bound to the chair like a rag doll. *Don't do it, Ashe*, he'd said, but I had to do it; giving the envelope back to Billy Rob was the only way I could get Tyler away from them.

Jimmy Connelly had been on their side all along. He'd told Billy Rob that I was going to the house in Rotherhithe. He'd pretended to be Tyler's friend. I thought back to the conversation we'd had a couple of days before, when he'd said that everything that had happened to Tyler had been my fault, had started with me. And all the while he knew that they had Tyler. How could he? *How could he?*

I stuck my hands far down into my pockets. In one of them were two mobile phones, in the other were my house keys, the trinkets attached to them wearing heavily through the fabric of my coat. I grabbed them tightly, squeezing my hand around them until it hurt.

I had to get home and get the envelope and wait for the

phone call. I realized that my lips were moving and I was talking aloud. I must have looked like a mad person. I closed my mouth and made myself concentrate. Get home. Pretend that nothing bad had happened. Pick up Tyler's envelope and wait for the phone call from Billy Rob.

I was nearing the station and I looked up.

Across the road, sitting on the taxi parking bay, was the silver Mini. The sight of it stopped me in my tracks. Florence with her long nails and her probing questions. Why was she there? How could it be that she was always around wherever I was? Was she following me?

The door opened and she got out and stood by the car.

I didn't know what to do. The tube entrance was straight ahead of me. I should walk towards it and get a train home and do what I had to do. And yet the thought of being on my own, of carrying the responsibility all alone was hard. Why not tell Florence?

I walked towards her.

"Get in," she said. "There's stuff we need to talk about."

That was it with Florence. There was always stuff to talk about.

I got in but she didn't start the car.

"I need to go home and pick up something," I said.

"You've been in the warehouse in Bryan Street."

She knew everything. She must have been hanging around Bryan Street, perhaps on the lookout for Billy Rob. She must have seen Jimmy and me.

"I've got to get home," I said, a little louder.

"How did you get into the building?"

"Are you going to take me home?" I demanded.

"I will. But first we have to have the truth! I'm fed up with you messing me around. How did you get into that building?"

"Keys."

"Did Tyler give you those keys? Is that what he gave you when you saw him in the hospital?"

I didn't answer. I felt weary and tired. I pulled both phones out of my pocket. I looked at the screen of mine. It was eight fifty. I had an hour and ten minutes until the phone call.

"You need to tell me what you know, Ashley."

"They've got Tyler in that building," I said.

Florence seemed to freeze. She stared at me. "He's not dead, though?" she whispered.

I shook my head. "No."

She sat back and made a slow whistling sound.

"But he might be if I don't get home!" I said, my voice cracking, feeling as though it had broken in half.

"OK, keep calm. I'll drive. But there's something you should know about me, Ashe. I'm a police officer."

I slumped back against the seat.

"What?"

I didn't need any more surprises.

"I'm an undercover police officer."

I stared at her. I shook my head in disbelief.

"You don't believe me?"

I didn't answer.

"Florence Monk is not my real name. This is a role I'm playing. Since the summer Tyler has been working for me, trying to find out if Martin Robertson had Joseph Lindsay killed."

"Oh," I said, my voice tiny.

"Now you need to tell me what you know. I want it all. The complete truth. From the beginning."

She started the car and pulled out into traffic.

I told her everything that had happened. I started with Tyler giving me the envelope. I described going to the police station and coming face to face with DI Brennan. I told her about overhearing Billy Rob talking about the *package* and going to Bryan Road that first time. She knew that, though; she had picked me up from the street after Billy Rob had seen me there. I explained about the envelope, looking at the memory stick and finding the CD. She got very excited at these things.

"You've still got this recording?" she said.

"You've got the photographs?" she said, later. "You've kept the CD with the recording? And the pictures of Robertson and Brennan together? You have it all. It's safe?"

"I've got the envelope in my house. It's on my computer as well. It's safe for now, but I have to give it to Billy Rob. Tonight. Otherwise he'll. . ."

I couldn't say it. I couldn't say the word *kill*.

"I'm sorry," I went on, "I know I've made a mess of it all. I should have told someone. Maybe if I had told Tyler's parents they could have done something. I've kept it a

162

complete secret. I've been lying to everyone. I haven't even told my best mate and she's Tyler's cousin."

"I'm sorry," she said, grabbing my hand and giving it a powerful squeeze. "I lied to you as well. Like you, I was doing it for the right reason. You did your best."

"We need to hurry. I've got to be ready for the phone call from Billy Rob. He's given me this mobile. I have to do it on my own but I don't feel like I can be on my own right now. I have to work up enough courage for this."

"You don't have to be alone. Not now. I'm here. We can finish this thing together."

Florence increased her speed. Then she started to explain her side of things even though I hadn't asked any questions or demanded any answers.

"I am part of a London-wide team that deal with drugs-related murders. See, if someone dies in suspicious circumstances in the world of drugs, there's not many who give a damn about it. The police usually think they got what they deserved and put their man-hours into other crime. My unit looks into unexplained deaths. Two years ago we looked at the case of Stuart Lister."

I was staring at my hands. I found it hard to concentrate. The news that Florence was not who she seemed to be was about as much as I could take. I kept glancing out of the window checking for familiar streets, hoping we would get back soon so that I could get the envelope and hold it tightly to my chest, keep it safe until Billy Rob told me where to take it. The name *Stuart Lister* resonated. Killed in a hit and run. Billy Rob had threatened my brother Dan with this knowledge, implying that there was more to it than just an accident.

"I don't want to go into too much detail, but Martin Robertson has about ten young men working for him, mostly as phone couriers, but they have other work as well. It makes them good money and it also makes them hard to catch. Delivering phones? Delivering drugs? It's a good cover. He also tries to get apprentices, young lads from school who start out using the stuff and then end up selling it."

We went across the river and were driving through the Docklands. We passed one apartment block after another. I noticed that it had started to rain, the drops skidding along the glass. Florence's voice was going on, but really I was thinking about what I had to do and whether it would turn out all right. In my head I pictured Tyler's envelope sitting in the drawer of my desk, covered with my schoolbooks.

"People like Martin Robertson keep their troops in line with money and perks, but occasionally there's one or two who think they can go it alone; get their drugs from a different source, earn more. That's where he has a problem."

"So he kills them," I said.

"Bluntly put but true. He doesn't just do it to get rid of them. He does it as an *example* to the rest of his workers. It's like saying, 'Look at what happened to Stuart Lister. You don't want that to happen to you.'"

I didn't have the energy to tell her about Dan.

"How long till we get home?" I said, edgily.

But Florence wasn't listening to me. She was caught up in her explanation.

"Drug dealers are hard to catch, Ashley. Very hard. They cover their tracks. But murder is a different thing. There's a trail with murder and it's up to my team to see if we can link it up."

Her team. It sounded like a game of netball.

"Joseph Lindsay got picked up for dealing last March. My team had access to him and we did a deal. We wanted him to find out anything we could about Martin and Billy Robertson. I pretended to be his girlfriend. I was around a lot and he fed me information. Then one night he was stabbed to death in a park. The officer on duty that night was a close friend of DI Norman Brennan. He investigated the case. He had a witness say that Joe was chased by three white men. They put the case down as a racist killing. As of yet not one person has been arrested."

I thought of the recorded conversation that was on the CD. The photos went along with it. It was all there, all the evidence that was needed to convict Martin Robertson. And he wanted it back.

"When Joe got killed Tyler was upset. He spun out of control for a while. Eventually I told him who I was and what I'd been doing. He agreed to help us. We worked together for almost three months but when nothing came out I was transferred on to another case. It was only in the last few days that I heard what had happened to him. If I'd been around, if he'd been able to reach me, he would have given the evidence in the envelope to me, but

I was undercover, on another job in Kent. No one could reach me."

I felt my chest deflate. I hadn't been Tyler's first choice after all. Amid all the grief I felt about what was happening that one fact seemed like a twist of the knife. He would have most certainly given the envelope to Florence, whatever her real name was.

We were nearing Bethnal Green. I stared at familiar territory. We passed by Jimmy's dad's shop, which was shut up. I wondered where Jimmy was and how he felt. I wondered if his pockets were full with thirty pieces of silver.

"This is all too much for you to take in in one go," Florence said, mistaking my despair for incomprehension.

She turned off the main road and headed for my street. I noticed then that she hadn't asked me for my address. How did she know so much about me? How was it that she seemed to be wherever I was? She pulled the car over and parked too early. My house was at the other end. Maybe I was wrong. Maybe she wasn't as knowledgeable as I thought.

I misread it, though. There was something she wanted to talk about.

"Ashley, you can't give that envelope back to Billy Robertson."

She called him Robertson, his full name. It made him sound less dangerous. I thought of a jar of jam, a name on a school register, Mr Robertson; a nice man. Billy *Rob* described him much better.

"It's evidence of a murder. You need to give that envelope to me."

"What about Tyler?" I said.

"We will rescue him."

"You don't know where he will be."

"No, but I'll be with you when you get the call at ten o'clock. You can tell me where they tell you to go. Then you go with a decoy envelope and an officer will follow until you have reached the destination."

You have reached the destination. It was what the satnav said whenever my mum's car reached home.

"When we know where they have Tyler then my team will get there. These are armed officers, Ashley. They will get him out."

"But meanwhile I'll be standing with a decoy envelope hoping that the police won't mess up."

"We won't mess up. We are professionals."

"What about Joseph Lindsay?"

She stiffened. I thought for a moment I'd made her angry.

"There isn't a day goes by that I don't think about Joseph Lindsay. We lost him, but we won't lose anyone else. Tyler is safe. You have my word for it."

I almost laughed. She sounded like someone out of a movie.

"And we'll get Marty and Billy and the rest of them."

I didn't answer. I didn't like the sound of it but I didn't want to argue with her.

"Will you do this? Will you work with us?"

I gave the tiniest of nods. It was better to agree.

"Good. I'll organize the things for the dummy envelope and be back at your house in thirty minutes. Is that OK?"

"No, meet me at the end of the street. Otherwise my parents will make a fuss."

"OK. In half an hour."

I nodded. I pushed the door open.

"I'll drive up to your door."

"No, I'll walk from here. I'll see you soon."

"It'll all work out, Ashley. I promise it will."

I nodded again. I watched her drive off. She was going to rescue Tyler and catch Martin Robertson. It was going to be a good night for her. Except that I had no intention of giving her the envelope and letting her know where Billy Rob wanted to meet me.

I was sticking to the plan.

It was up to the police to get to Marty Robertson on their own.

My responsibility was to get Tyler back from Billy Rob.

TWENTY-TWO

I opened my front door as quietly as I could. The sound of the television was coming from the living room. The kitchen was in darkness so I guessed my mum and dad were watching a programme together. I went quickly up to my bedroom. I took my phone and Billy Rob's pay as you go and placed them side by side on the bed. I took my keys and my travel card out and placed them alongside. I wanted to have everything that I needed ready.

My laptop was still open from the afternoon. I pressed the on button and listened as it came back to life. Back then I had been looking at the photos and listening to the recording. I'd been excited because I'd made a discovery. Then I was just playing around with things, being a detective. Now, hours later, I was trying to save Tyler's life. Now I had to close it down, take it with me to Billy Rob and he would destroy it, I was sure. It didn't matter to me.

The only thing that mattered was that they let Tyler go.

I got the envelope out. I tipped it on to the bed again and looked at the things. My heart was thumping as I picked up each item and held it for a moment. Then I sat down. The minutes were ticking away but I was suddenly stricken, not able to move, to make plans, to organize myself. I sat on the bed surrounded by objects that had suddenly become a matter of life or death. It weighed heavily on me. I didn't want to move. I wanted to lie down, pull the duvet up and let time pass so that I was not responsible for what was going to happen.

I glanced at my laptop and then looked again at the things on the bed; then I picked my bunch of keys up and cradled it against my neck, feeling the sharpness of the serrations and the points of the letter A digging into my flesh.

I used my fingers to feel out the memory stick that Dan had bought for me. I held it in front of me. Billy Rob wanted to see my laptop. He most certainly would not give it back to me. It would be the price I paid for getting Tyler back. Then the evidence would be gone. I sat down at the table and unhooked the gold memory stick. I plugged it into the side of my laptop. It only took a moment to save the CD and the photographs. I took it out and fed it back on to my key ring.

I closed the laptop down, my mouth dry.

When I finally got everything back in the envelope I put it inside my rucksack. Then I slid the laptop in. I put my coat on and picked up my keys and my travel card from the bed.

There was a light knock on the door and Dan came in.

"Where have you been? Beth was round."

"I had something to do."

"She seems a bit upset. She says she thinks there's something up with you. Something about Tyler Harrington."

"It's nothing," I said.

"Are you sure? You look a bit odd."

"No, really. I've just got something to sort out."

I glanced over at my bedside clock. It was twenty past nine. I wanted to get out of the house so that I could be far away before Florence realized that I hadn't turned up and came looking for me. I needed money from the cash machine for a taxi. Tyler had looked dreadful. I didn't think he'd be able to walk.

Dan had said something and was waiting for an answer.

"What?" I said.

"Beth thinks you're being distant."

"I can't talk now," I said, putting my hand on his arm and edging him towards the door. "Really, right this moment I can't talk. I will talk to you later, tomorrow. And Beth too."

He turned to go but looked back at me doing my coat up.

"You going out? At this time?"

I nodded.

"Does Mum know?"

I shook my head. I hadn't thought about my mum. "No. Look, could you give her a message from me? Tell her I'm staying round Beth's tonight and then ring Beth and tell her what you've told Mum in case she rings. Will you do that for me?"

"But where are you going?"

I was getting angry. I had my eye on the time and I was trying to remember the things I wanted to take and Dan was in my face asking me questions when I didn't need it. All the time I was aware that Florence might get back early, might be sitting in the silver Mini at the end of the road waiting for me.

"Do you remember last year? When you had trouble with Billy Rob?"

He nodded, his face creased up.

"I helped you then. Do you remember?"

"Course."

"I'm asking you to help me now."

I could hear the sound of the living room door opening from downstairs. Mum or Dad was coming out of the room. If Mum came up here she would want to know what was happening and it wouldn't be easy to get out. She wouldn't let it go. She'd stop me somehow. I began to feel panicky.

"I don't want Mum to know I'm here. Don't ask me why! Just go downstairs. Distract her for five minutes and then tell her I phoned earlier and said I was staying at Beth's. Please?"

"How am I going to distract her?"

"Have a heart to heart with her about your plans. I don't know!"

"You've got to be kidding. . ." he started, but stopped when he saw my face harden.

"Go now! Please!" I said.

He went. I heard his footsteps down the stairs. I listened hard. I heard his voice and then Mum's voice; then a few moments later I heard the kitchen door shutting. I breathed easier. I picked up the rucksack, heavier now that it had my laptop in it. I went out of my room. I slipped downstairs, hoping my dad wouldn't suddenly appear at the living room door. He didn't. I opened the front door and shut it as quietly as I could. I looked down the end of the street but I couldn't see the silver Mini. In any case I turned in the opposite direction and took the long way to the tube.

I stopped at the cash machine and withdrew a hundred pounds. Ten minutes later I was on a tube heading for Stratford. When I got there I stayed on the platform. I sat on a bench, held Billy Rob's pay as you go mobile in my hand and waited for his call.

At three minutes past ten the mobile rang.

"Listen carefully," a voice said. "I want you to go to Mile End Station. Someone will be waiting for you there."

The call ended. The voice was Billy Rob's, I was sure. I walked across to the opposite platform and got on a tube going the other way. In minutes I was at Mile End Station. I walked up the stairs and went through the ticket machine and out on to the street. The area was busy still, people milling round, looking as though they had places to go, things to do. I looked up the road and saw the neon lights of the Foneswapshop. Then I heard the hoot of a car horn. Across the road, parked on the zigzag lines of the pelican crossing, was the BMW I had seen the other night. I couldn't see who was in the driver's seat. I took a step towards it and faltered because something awful occurred to me.

What's to stop them just taking the stuff off me now? I thought. If I got in the car and went with them why should they keep their end of the bargain? They could just take my bag off me. How could I fight them? I stood uncertainly for a moment. I put one foot forward but the ground beneath me seemed to veer away.

The horn hooted again, a little more impatiently this time.

I thought hard. I needed a story. I needed some reason for them not to mess around with me. I walked slowly towards the car. I was surprised when the driver's door opened and Marty Robertson got out.

The sight of him made me feel better.

Marty Robertson was an older man, like someone's dad or uncle. He didn't look like someone who would do bad things. Possibly it was Billy Rob who was the out-of-control one and Marty, his dad, was clearing up his mess. Maybe he had come along to make sure things were going to go right. Then I remembered his voice on the tape talking about the money he had paid to DI Brennan. *Make the most of it. That should be the last problem I have for a while.* Possibly he was there precisely to make sure that nothing went wrong and no one got hurt.

"All right, dear?" Marty Robertson said as I got closer.

I walked round the other side of the car as he got back in. I screwed up my courage and got into the car. When I was sitting in the passenger's seat I spoke.

"I've told a friend where I am. She's a policewoman. She expects me to contact her when Tyler is safe."

I held my breath, expecting him to be angry.

"All right, dear."

As we drove off I thought, miserably, *Why didn't I let Florence follow me?*

Music filled the car. It was an old-fashioned sound, a man singing a ballad, lots of orchestra behind him.

"*Phantom of the Opera*," Marty Robertson said.

I nodded, feeling strange and awkward. He didn't sound like a dangerous man and yet the fact that he was involved in this at all meant that he was. He drove slowly and carefully and we seemed to be heading into the city. I wondered where we were going. I crossed my legs and uncrossed them. I swallowed, my mouth feeling papery, wishing I'd brought a bottle of water with me. We passed the Tower of London. I stared at its squat silhouette, the dark sky beyond it. It had started to rain again, lightly this time, barely noticeable except under the street lights. The song changed and a woman started to sing. Marty Robertson began to hum.

"Where are we going?" I said.

"St Paul's," he said and went back to humming.

I wondered what Florence was doing. She'd known for a while that I had given her the slip. I wondered if she'd gone to my house to find me. I hoped not. Maybe she would go to the shop on Mile End Road or back to Bryan Street to see if any evidence or clues had been left behind.

Up ahead I could see the great dome of St Paul's. The outline of it was just visible against the dark sky. The windows were wet, the rain coming down more steadily.

The windscreen wipers swept the drops away, giving clear vision for seconds before the rain dotted the screen again. I watched them go to and fro, swinging back and forth, making a fan shape on the glass. It was making me feel light-headed so I closed my eyes and counted to ten. Then I did it backwards.

How long until this was all over?

I felt the car turn a corner. We were going downhill; the streets were cobbled, uneven. I could see the Millennium Bridge ahead of me and beyond that, on the other side of the river, the Tate Modern building, its giant tower thrusting up, disappearing into the night sky.

The car slowed down, turning again. I lost sight of the bridge but I knew we were travelling parallel to the river. We went on for about twenty metres and then stopped.

"Here we are, my dear."

I got out of the car, my legs feeling weak. Across the road was a wharf. A sign by it said *St Paul's Thames Waterbus*. There was a ticket machine and some benches and a walkway out on to the river, but it was all closed up. When I looked down, over the side I saw a number of small boats moored there. At the end was a much larger one. It was the type of boat that took tourists up and down the river. Only this end of it had a light; the rest of it was in darkness. On the boarding deck I could see Billy Rob in his black jeans and jacket. Phil was beside him. Behind them, out of the light, it was all in shadow. My eyes scanned the area but I couldn't see the other man, Scot, nor could I see Tyler.

Billy Rob beckoned to me to approach and I walked down the Thames Waterbus steps and on to a concrete jetty. I forced myself forward, aware of the precarious situation I was in. I heard Marty Robertson coming behind me. I slowed down as I stepped on a wooden walkway and passed by half-a-dozen boats. The tourist boat was at the end and I could still only see Billy Rob and Phil on the deck. It was a single-level boat. Only the rear lights were on, the rest was black. I could see its name painted on the side in italics, *Anne Boleyn.*

"Right on time!" Billy Rob said. "Come aboard."

"I've told a policewoman where I am! They've probably followed me here."

As the words came out I realized how ridiculous it sounded. How could anyone know where I was when I hadn't known myself? It was just bravado. I felt feeble and pathetic as I put one foot on to the gangplank. I wobbled a bit and Phil put his hand out to steady me. I stepped down into the boat and stood with my arms crossed, both hands holding on to some part of the rucksack that I had brought.

"Where's Tyler?" I said.

Billy Rob lifted up the torch he had taken from me earlier. He shone it into the dark part of the boat. Tyler was sitting down, gagged again. Scot was behind him.

"Now," Billy Rob said, "you've got something to give me first."

"What about Tyler?" I said.

"You first."

I unzipped the bag and pulled out the envelope. I avoided looking at Tyler and held on to it for a moment. Then I handed it over. Billy Rob looked at it for a few seconds; then he began to laugh.

"And the rest!"

I pulled the laptop out and held it like a tray in my hands. Phil took it from me.

"Thanks, Tyler!" Billy Rob called, letting the torch zigzag across the black interior of the boat, catching Tyler's face for a second.

My stomach folded.

I knew, in that moment, that he wasn't going to let Tyler go.

I felt the boat starting up and realized that we were moving off, away from dry land and out into the river.

TWENTY-THREE

The boat see-sawed in the water and drifted out away from the riverbank. The engine rumbled and I looked to see that a light had gone on up the other end and Scot was sitting in an elevated seat, steering. Tyler had been left on one of the tourist benches.

There was an icy blast of wind and I had to steady myself. I felt my feet scrabbling about, but someone grabbed my shoulder. It was Phil. He held me firmly while Billy Rob opened the envelope. We were getting further away from the jetty as he pulled out the CD and the memory stick. He walked over to the side of the boat and flung them both into the water.

"Thank you for this. It doesn't change anything, but it's good to have it back."

Then he tossed the envelope over the side.

"You said you would let Tyler go!"

"I lied."

"We won't say anything. Tyler won't say anything. . ."

"No. After tonight he won't say anything."

Phil handed my laptop to him. He looked it over as though he were a customer in a shop.

"Cheap rubbish," he said.

He didn't bother to open it up, check to see if I'd copied anything. He held it like a Frisbee. Then he threw it out of the boat. It rose up before it disappeared over the side. I didn't even hear a splash.

"Mobile," he said.

I got my phone and the pay-as-you-go one out of my pocket. He snatched them from me and tossed them out of the boat.

"Please don't hurt Tyler," I said.

"I'm not going to *hurt* him. He's just going to go for a swim."

I felt a swooning feeling, but steadied myself as the boat seemed to dip to one side. I looked round and saw that we were being overtaken by a bigger tourist boat. A river cruiser. It had two floors and was lit up, sending out a glow across the water. I could see people inside sitting at dinner tables. I wanted to put my hand up and wave but there was no one looking in our direction. I thought of calling out but the noise of its engines was deafening.

"Careful, my dear. We don't want you to get seasick," Marty Robertson said, grabbing hold of my coat and pulling me back from the edge.

"The police will be here soon," I said, pulling myself together, trying to sound positive. "They know where I am. They've been following me ever since Mile End. They know this case. You've been under surveillance for months."

Billy Rob shook his head. I felt Marty Robertson's fingers tightening on my arm.

"No. No one followed you. Don't you think we check those things?"

"Please don't do anything to Tyler. Otherwise. . ."

"Otherwise what?"

"*I* will go to police. I'll tell them everything. I'll be a witness."

"No you won't," he said.

I stared at him. I could taste the tears on my lips. I wiped them away with the back of my hand and shrugged Marty Robertson's arm off. The cruise boat was moving away from us. The choppy water fanned out behind it and we were caught in its wake. The boat went up and down as though it was going over speed humps and Phil and Billy Rob grabbed on to the deck rail. From behind I could hear Phil laughing.

"I will tell the police," I said, my voice dropping.

"Trust me, my dear. You won't say a word. You will be as quiet as the grave."

I couldn't take my eyes off him. He was ugly, his mouth a dark gash in his face. His smart jacket and crisply ironed jeans, his cocky smile and his polite ways covered up a black heart. Had he been one of the men who stabbed Joseph Lindsay? Who'd chased him into a park in the dead of night? Or had he been behind the steering wheel of the car that hit Stuart Lister early one morning?

"Phil, get her ready."

I turned and saw Phil pull out a length of rope.

I suddenly understood. Marty Robertson could have taken the envelope and the laptop off me at Mile End and driven away with it. He could have left me standing on the road, a stupid girl who had no idea what sort of people she was dealing with. A simple push to the shoulder and I would have stumbled away and watched the rear lights of his car disappear up the road towards the city. But he hadn't. He'd taken me with him all the way to St Paul's. All the way on to the *Anne Boleyn*. I was to rescue Tyler. To do an exchange, but that had never been part of any plan. They were not going to let Tyler go and now that they knew that I was involved, that I knew about the envelope and its contents, they were not going to let me go either.

They were violent people who stopped at nothing.

The boat veered unexpectedly to the side and I stumbled. I grabbed hold of a post and steadied myself.

"Careful," Billy Rob said with a smirk. "You don't want to get hurt."

I closed my eyes to stop the tears.

They were going to kill us both.

TWENTY-FOUR

The river looked black but for the shimmer of the moon picking up eddies across the surface. I looked up and saw the bright lights of the cruise boat moving away from us and felt colder than I ever had in my life. My breath formed in little puffs and my lips felt caked and hard.

I closed my eyes and felt like I was falling down a dark hole.

"Now, you need to be clear about this," Billy Rob said. "What we'll do tonight is not something we enjoy. We do it because we have to. Once it's over we'll go home and get back to work. We take no pleasure in it. The black copper'll be in the dark. Like she has been for a long while."

My shoulders sagged. *The black copper*. They knew about Florence Monk.

We were passing under Tower Bridge. The boat was low down. It felt like the city was high above us; millions of people going about their business unaware of what was happening down on the river. I looked up at the giant struts and felt completely helpless. Why hadn't I waited for Florence? What had I thought I was doing?

"Now you can go and sit with your boyfriend. It won't

be long until we get to the right place. Then we can get this over with and go home."

Phil tied my hands together in front of me. Then he led me into the covered section of the boat. I shook his hand off and sat down beside Tyler. Scot must have taken the gag off because it was sitting crumpled on the seat beside him. His wrists were tied like mine. He looked terrible. The cut at the side of his eye looked bigger like a gaping mouth. I lifted my hands and tried to touch his arm. It felt hot, searing, as though he had a fever.

"They'll let us go," I whispered, "they will. This is just to frighten us."

He shook his head.

"You don't know them."

"No, I heard them arguing," I lied, "they're not sure what to do."

I stifled a sob. I needed a tissue. As I shifted about I felt the weight of my bunch of keys in my pocket. I pictured the gold memory stick sitting among all my childhood fobs. I'd saved the data on it hours before, thinking I would be able to give it to Florence after it was all over. How naïve I had been. *Stupid, stupid.*

"I'm sorry," I said. "If I'd just kept the envelope safe. . ."

"I don't blame you."

The engine was chugging along. The boat sounded as though it was weary. I looked at the three men standing at the back. They seemed normal, some friends on a night out. They weren't, though; they intended to kill us. I felt a sob coming out of my mouth.

184

"Florence knows," I said.

"What?" he said, looking brighter. "She's in on this? She's following you? She knows where we are?"

"I think so," I said.

It was a downright lie but I said it anyway.

"Maybe she'll get here. Maybe she'll alert the river police. We might be all right."

He seemed to be trembling. I wanted to put my arm round him but I couldn't. I leaned my shoulder into his and put my head near his neck. The men were in a huddle. Phil kept pointing to the riverbank and I thought, *They're looking for a place to pull in and kill us.* I got as close to Tyler as I could. My forehead was touching his cheek. For the first time in almost a year I was beside him, close to him when it was too late to matter. Up ahead I could see the lights of Canary Wharf, the giant towers lit up amid the black surrounds of docklands. We moved slowly along and he seemed to slump towards me, as if he was falling asleep.

I nudged him. He had to keep alert. We might have a chance of fighting them off or making a scene and alerting someone on the riverbank or on the water. We had to be awake and focused. In any case I had things to say to him.

"I'm so sorry about last Christmas. I never knew what you did for my brother."

He shook his head.

"I saw you in Alexandra Drive, I just jumped to conclusions. . ."

"Ssh. . ." he said.

"I'll never forget what you did," I said.

"Jimmy tell you?"

I nodded.

"Good mate Jimmy."

I looked at him, puzzled. Did he not know about Jimmy? His eyes were closing and he was leaning heavily on me.

"What happened in the hospital?" I said, to keep him from drifting away.

"Billy Rob came for me."

"Why did you go with him?"

"He had Jimmy's mobile. He said he was holding Jimmy. He said if I went quietly he would let him go. At least that worked out. At least Jimmy's not a victim in this."

I didn't answer. I didn't think it was possible for Jimmy to sink lower in my estimation. I opened my mouth to tell Tyler but then I thought, *What is the point? Why upset him any more?*

I kept talking quietly, trying to keep him awake. My hands were on top of his. We didn't seem to be getting any closer to the lights of Canary Wharf, just further into the darkness. I felt his fingers moving under my hand.

"See if you can fiddle with the rope. You might be able to loosen it," I whispered.

"The Great Escape," he said, giving a dismal laugh.

"Do it," I said, my mouth next to his ear.

I felt his fingers toying with the rope, pulling it, teasing it; after a while he was able to slip a finger between my hand and the rope. He seemed to flag then.

"Keep going!" I said.

I could hear the sound of traffic in the distance. A siren was going. It flew past us, getting louder and then fading into the distance. I kept my eye on the men, waiting for them to move towards us. The river was bending. The wind snaked into the covered area and chilled me. Tyler didn't notice. He was burning up.

Then I saw the weights. They were in a holdall down by Tyler's feet. It had been unzipped and I could see the chunky metal rings lined up side by side.

They really meant it. I felt myself shrinking into my seat.

"What's up?" Tyler said, in a husky voice.

"Nothing," I squeaked.

"Keep your eyes open for the river police," he said, pulling at the rope around my wrists.

"I will. I'll keep looking," I said, hopelessly, tears streaming down my face.

"Tell me if you see them."

"I will. I'll tell you."

I found myself staring at the opposite bank of the river, looking among the shadows for a boat that might thrust out and speed across the river towards us. There was no point but I searched the surface of the water anyway. I could feel Tyler pulling at the rope, making a gap big enough to slip the palm of his hand through. He took his hand away. The rope had loosened. I could slip it off if I wanted. I held it in place with my fingers. I didn't want any of the men to notice. Tyler leaned into me, his head on my neck. I felt him trembling and heard him sniffing. I knew he was crying.

"Keep strong," I said. "When it stops I will try and fight them. You run at one of them. Maybe we can throw them off guard."

"It's too late," he said, "I'm too tired."

"No, it's not too late," I said.

There was a lurch and the engine stopped.

The boat floated directionless and I felt this frisson of fear. I sat very still. I was swallowing over and over. Was there any possibility that I could fight them off? I glanced down at the weights in the bag by our feet. Could I cause a scene that someone, maybe on another boat, would notice? I looked across the dark water. There was a dredger in the middle of the river and a yacht further away.

"Any sign of Flo?" Tyler said.

"Not yet."

The lights went off on the boat. We were in complete darkness. Billy Rob was walking towards us. From behind I could hear footsteps. Scot had come back. I looked at the weights. As Scot got closer I made a decision. I waited until he reached out for Tyler's arm and I edged off the rope and scooped up one of the weights. He was startled. I held the weight as tightly as I could and hit out at Scot, at the side of his face, two, three times. He shouted out and veered back. Then I threw it at Billy Rob and it hit him on the shoulder and it clattered on to the deck and skidded along the floor.

Then Billy Rob was next to me. He swore loudly and grabbed my jacket at the neck and threw me across the boat. I hit my back against the side and fell forward on to the deck.

I looked up. They had Tyler.

"Him first, then her," Billy Rob said.

They were going to kill us and I couldn't do a single thing about it.

TWENTY-FIVE

Billy Rob and Phil were holding Tyler while Scot tied the gag around his mouth. He had to struggle because Tyler was twisting his head back and forth. Then he put weights into Tyler's jacket pockets. They slid in and clunked against each other. I managed to get to my feet and I made a run at them. I used my fists to hit at Billy Rob's back. He swatted me away and I stumbled to the side of the boat.

"Help, help, HELP!" I screamed, leaning over the water, throwing my voice as far as I could into the blackness.

Phil stepped across and grabbed me from behind. He held me in an armlock and put the flat of his hand across my mouth. I struggled as he turned me round. Tyler was thrashing about, moving his plastered foot as if to kick out. Phil relaxed his hand for a second and I bit into it. He let me go and I lunged towards Billy Rob and grabbed his jacket and tried to pull him away from Tyler but he swiped me away and I stumbled backwards and fell, hitting my head. For a second I lay there. My vision was dappled, my head numb; then I felt a sharp pain. I wanted to close my eyes and black it all out but I knew I couldn't.

There were mumblings coming from Tyler and I heard Billy Rob swearing quietly. Then it went quiet. There wasn't a sound. The three of them had hold of Tyler and were edging him towards the rear of the boat. He was turning from one side to the other and they were heaving him along. Marty Robertson was standing away from them, looking serene as if he was watching a game.

For a second there was silence. I held my breath. This was when they were going to do it; to throw Tyler over the side of the boat. I expected to hear a splash.

Instead I heard a siren.

It was a wail that came out of the blackness; a banshee, a ghost from the riverbank. It was coming closer, moving towards us. I got up, my head stinging from where I'd knocked it, and I looked out towards the north bank of the River Thames, expecting to see a squad car or a van, a flashing blue light racing towards us. But there was nothing.

It was coming from the other side of the river.

"Quick, quick," Billy Rob was saying.

But Phil and Scot had stood back.

I looked out at the river. It was a *boat* that was heading for us. The siren was coming from it but there was no spinning light on the top. Instead there was a giant beam in front of it. A floodlight which lit up a V-shaped chunk of the river.

It *was* a police boat.

Where had it come from? What had it seen? How did it know that we were there?

"Come on," Billy Rob was urging the others, but they were standing back looking shocked.

"Pull yourself together, Billy," Marty Robertson said. "This little joke we've been having with Tyler is over. Are you all right, son? You do know it was a joke? We never intended to do anything, right?"

Billy Rob flung Tyler away from him and Tyler fell on to the deck. I rushed over to him. I pulled at his gag and scrabbled about in his pockets for the weights. Then I tried to untie his hands. The rope was tight, though, too tight for me to get my finger underneath.

The police boat siren had stopped. It was metres away, the beam of light illuminating our boat. It bobbed up and down in the water. There was a policeman on the bow of the boat. He put his hands on either side of his mouth and shouted.

"This is the Metropolitan Marine Support Unit. I'm instructing you to stand still, not to operate your vessel, and keep your hands at your sides while my officers board and speak with you."

"We need an ambulance!" I called out. "An ambulance."

"You have an injured party?"

"Yes!"

I pointed to Tyler.

Phil and Scot stood together. They looked uncomfortable but Marty Robertson and Billy Rob were smiling.

"There's nothing to link us with any crimes," Billy Rob said.

"A bit of horseplay that got out of hand," Marty Robertson said.

I saw something else approaching across the river. It

had a light on it but nothing as bright as the river police boat. It was coming at speed, the front of it raised up out of the water. I strained my eyes to see and realized that it was another police boat, an inflatable speedboat. It disturbed the water and made the first boat rock and sent waves towards us. There was someone driving the boat but I could also see someone standing up, with binoculars, looking in our direction.

When the boat got closer I could see who it was.

Florence Monk.

She had found me. She had been there to rescue Tyler like she'd said she would. How she had done it I didn't know, but she had been true to her word.

TWENTY-SIX

They took Tyler off first.

I watched him being hoisted from boat to boat on a stretcher. The police had moved the four men to the far end of the boat and I was sitting next to Florence, who had found me an old red blanket and put it round my shoulders. My teeth were chattering and I was trying to speak, but she told me, in a soothing voice, to be quiet.

When Tyler was safely across she helped me stand up. She passed me on to a river policeman who gave me a life jacket and helped me put it on. I held on to the red blanket, tucking it round my neck. Then with the help of another officer he lifted me on to the side. The police boat was parallel and roped to the *Anne Boleyn*. It left a narrow gap and I could see the river below.

"Are you OK?" the policeman said. "We can hoist you if you'd rather."

I shook my head. All I had to do was step across. There were two officers waiting with their arms out to steer me aboard. It was noisy, the engine of the police boat loud and commanding. The officers were shouting to each other, their words colliding. I didn't look down. The swell of the water meant that the police boat was momentarily higher than the one I was on. Then it dipped. I took a deep breath and stepped across. One of my arms was still being held from behind and as I went to put my foot down the police boat dipped again and an alarming gap opened up between the two boats and I was distracted by the noise of sirens and dazzling blue lights from across the river. Suddenly it was all too much and my legs went to jelly. I seemed to lose my balance and tipped backwards and felt a policeman's hands stopping me from falling. The red blanket dropped off. I tried to grab it but I was concentrating on catching hold of the other policeman's hand and I had to let it go. I steadied myself and stood upright and stepped into the police boat. I turned and looked down. The red blanket was in the water. I was shaken and my steps were wobbly but I was led across the deck to a seat. Another officer put a silver thermal blanket around me.

The ambulance was at the jetty. Florence led me to the silver Mini. An ambulance man had a quick look at me but I assured him I was fine, cuts and bruises only. I watched the others carry Tyler's stretcher to the back doors of the ambulance and carefully feed him in. The doors closed gently and then it moved away cautiously, as though it had a fragile cargo. The light flashed, making the jetty blue for a second; then it was gone.

Marty Robertson, Billy Rob, Phil and Scot were still on the *Anne Boleyn* on the other side of the river. After a few moments talking to officers and making calls Florence got into the car and we drove off. I'd been so keen to talk when I was on the *Anne Boleyn*, but now I had no words to say and just pulled the thermal blanket around me and stared straight ahead.

"I had a feeling you wouldn't wait for me," Florence said. "I knew even as I was putting together the fake envelope that you wouldn't show up," she said, blowing through her teeth. "I'm not angry at you, though. You did your best. You probably saved Tyler's life."

You saved him, not me, I wanted to say but simply didn't have the strength.

She talked on about how she'd contacted her team and they'd liaised with the river police. She explained how it had been tricky because the river police were a law unto themselves and were not good at collaborating with other units.

"They like to be in charge," Florence said. "They like to have the glory. They don't like other units using them to make arrests. But they have jurisdiction on the river, so we had no choice but to work with them. My guv'nor knows someone high up. Went to the same boarding school together or something like that. He rang them and then, Hey presto! Everything moved into place. They had you in their sights before you left St Paul's."

We were moving in and out of the late evening traffic. I was staring out of the window, my eyes blurring at the different colours blinking at me out of the darkness: traffic lights, car lights, neon signs, Christmas tree decorations, flickering bulbs that hung like bunting from lamp post to lamp post. Then, when my eyes swivelled back into the car and looked along the dashboard the indicator light pulsed at me and the dials glowed warmly.

Something was bothering me. Underneath all the spent tension and anxiety of the last couple of hours something else was nagging at me.

"It won't be long until I get you to the hospital," Florence said, as if she'd just noticed that I was flagging.

I looked at her profile, her mahogany skin standing out against the muddy interior of the car. Her hair was pulled back in a bunch, curls escaping at the base of her neck. She had studs on again but I couldn't tell what colour. At first I hadn't liked her, hadn't trusted her, but she'd done what she said, she'd rescued Tyler when I had been no good at all.

I knew then what was niggling me.

"How did you find me?" I said, my voice croaking. "How did you know I was on a boat on the river?"

"GPS," she said.

I frowned.

"Global Positioning Satellite."

"What's that?"

"Satellite navigation. Every time you moved it showed up on a screen. I knew where you were. I attached a tiny device to your bunch of keys, this morning, in the supermarket café."

I was still puzzled.

"I knew you weren't going to confide in me and I didn't have time to wait you out. I needed to know where you were going. I thought you probably wouldn't notice it. Well, I hoped you wouldn't."

She had been following me via a satellite.

"It's attached by magnet," she continued.

It was a charm. It was magic. Something up in space had saved our lives. I shuffled about on the seat and felt for my key fobs. They weren't in the pocket where I usually kept them. I frowned. I tried my other pocket. That too was empty. I felt around on the seat beneath but they weren't there.

They were gone.

I tried again. Nothing.

I unfastened my seat belt and bent down to feel in the well of the seat, moving my feet to see if they had dropped, hoping to hear a reassuring tinkling sound.

They weren't there.

"You all right?" Florence said.

I began to cry quietly.

Florence put her hand out and grabbed mine. I felt her long nails against my skin as she gripped me.

"It's all over now, Ashley. Everything's all right. We'll be at A and E soon."

Florence took me straight past the waiting area and into the treatment rooms. I sat in a cubicle, a curtain pulled around to shield me off. A doctor saw me quickly. He took my blood pressure and looked me over, taking a few minutes to examine my head where I'd fallen on the *Anne Boleyn*. He told me to lie back. He was worried about shock and wanted to monitor me for a while. Florence went off to get a hot drink and I asked her to find out about Tyler. When I was on my own I pulled my knees up and hugged myself. My clothes smelled of brine and made me think of the thick, dark, choppy waters of the Thames, and I felt a thrust of fear at what might have happened.

Stupid, stupid.

How close it had been to a disaster.

And now my keys were lost, perhaps dropped into the sea when I stumbled getting from boat to boat. The key fobs all gone; childish things that should have been put away in a drawer years ago. But that wasn't what was important. The memory stick had gone. That evening, before going to meet Billy Rob, before giving up the evidence in exchange for Tyler, I had saved it all on the memory stick which Dan had bought me. Now, like the laptop and the contents of the envelope, it was sitting on the bottom of the river.

I turned my face into the crisp hospital pillow. I could smell salt and I closed my eyes, picturing the gawdy key fobs sinking slowly through the black water; my initial A, the Eiffel Tower bought on a trip to Paris, the silver heart, a present from my mum. All of it coming to rest on the river bed. In among them the gold memory stick that held the evidence that would have put Marty Robertson and Billy Rob and DI Brennan in prison.

TWENTY-SEVEN

After what seemed like a long while Florence came back with a paper cup of hot sweet tea. She gave it to me and I took a mouthful. Outside the cubicle it had gone quiet. I could hear voices from far away and the creak of moving trolleys but it all sounded hushed. I wondered what the time was. I patted my pocket for my phone but remembered that I didn't have that any more.

"It's ten to one," Florence said when I asked.

"Did you see Tyler?"

"He's been admitted. He's in a side room in Victoria Ward. They're putting him under observation for tonight and tomorrow they'll do some X-rays and blood tests and see whether his condition has worsened. Meanwhile he's sedated and on a drip. He'll probably sleep for a week."

I nodded.

"He'll be fine."

"What about Marty Robertson? And Billy Rob? Will they be charged with Tyler's abduction? Attempted murder?"

"Possibly. They're saying it was a prank that went wrong. They're saying that Tyler left hospital willingly and went with them independently. It's four people's word against Tyler. We might be able to swing a deal. You know, drop the attempted murder charge and get them for false imprisonment."

"But what about my evidence? I was there. I saw what they were going to do."

"We'll be able to charge them with something. But these people have expensive lawyers and. . ."

"What about Stuart Lister and Joseph Lindsay?"

"I doubt we'll be able to do much about those cases. The evidence is gone. It's sitting at the bottom of the Thames."

I couldn't bring myself to tell her about the key fobs. What was the point?

"There's one other possibility. In the morning I'm going to speak to DI Brennan. I'm going to try and pressure him by telling him about the photos and the recording and your evidence. None of it will stand up in court, but it might be possible to make a deal with him. My boss says that maybe he could quietly resign from the police in return for his evidence."

"Then he gets away with it?"

"But then we get Marty Roberston and his son. It's the way of the world, Ashley. I'll be in touch."

As she walked out, I realized that she looked smaller. She was wearing flat shoes instead of the killer heels I had seen her in. She must have changed at some point. Or maybe she always had the flats in her car and heels were part of the persona she had taken on. It made me feel sad that Florence was fading away.

My mum and dad came soon after. Dan arrived within minutes of them.

My mum looked pale and upset. My dad seemed awkward and out of place, standing away from the bed. He hardly said a word while my mum cross-examined me about what happened. All the while she gripped on to one of my arms, feeling up and down as if to make sure my bones were in one piece. They spoke at length to the doctor, who said I'd had a shock and just needed a warm bed and some paracetamol for the bump on my head.

He said I could go home.

When we were ready to leave I asked them if it was all right for me to go up to the ward and see Tyler.

"It's the middle of the night!" my mum said, testily.

"I just want to have a look at him. To make sure he's OK."

My mum grudgingly agreed and said they'd get the car and wait for me outside. Dan insisted on coming with me. All the way in the lift he held my arm.

"Is this something to do with what happened last year?" he said. "With Billy Rob and the drugs?"

I nodded. There was no point in lying. Not now. I felt him slacken and saw him shaking his head.

"I told you not to get involved. I told you I'd do what I had to do then it would all have been finished."

"Maybe for you it would, but what about other people? Other lads? Two boys are dead. Tyler nearly died. And I..."

I wanted to say *I could have been next* but I didn't.

The lift stopped. Dan put his arm round my shoulder.

"Oh, sis," he said, "what did I get you into?"

I walked on. "It's over now," I said.

The hospital corridor was deserted. Outside it was pitch black. From far away I could hear the sound of someone shouting. It startled me. A single voice, angry and loud. Then it stopped. We walked on. We got as far as the doors to Victoria Ward and I hesitated. Why was I doing this? It was me who got Tyler into this in the first place. It changed his life and he almost got killed.

"Are you going in?" Dan said.

"I don't know," I said.

I remembered those terrible moments when the boat slopped from side to side, when Billy Rob, Scot and Phil pulled Tyler towards the water. I was lying on the deck looking up, not able to do anything.

Why would he want anything to do with me?

"Changed my mind," I said, "it's too late. It might disturb someone."

I turned back to the lift and Dan followed me.

We walked out of the hospital into the car park. It was almost empty. There were a few cars parked close to the main entrance but Mum and Dad's was in the middle, on its own. I was desperately tired. I wanted to go home, to be on my own. I walked ahead of Dan towards the car. Halfway across the car park I heard someone shout my name.

"Ashley Littlewood!"

I turned and saw a uniformed police officer hurrying towards me.

"Are you Ashley Littlewood?" he said when he got close.

"Yes."

"I'm glad I caught you. My DI asked me to give you these. She says they're definitely yours."

He was holding out my key fobs. They hung from his hand. I looked at them in amazement.

"They are yours? My DI said she was sure. We found them on the deck of the *Anne Boleyn*."

I took them from him, my mouth breaking into a smile.

"They weren't in the water?"

"No, I picked them up myself. They were under one of the seats in the covered part of the boat. I thought they were evidence at first but my DI says not. She says they are yours."

I took them. They felt heavy and warm. I squeezed my hand around them and felt the familiar jags on my skin. I opened my palm and they lay there while I sorted through for the memory stick. There it was, gold and slim like a posh lipstick.

"Where is she? The DI? Is she still here?" I said, looking round the car park, hoping to see Florence's face somewhere.

"She's just about to leave."

"Where is her car parked?"

"Erm . . . not sure."

"I have to find her," I said. "This is really important. It's about some evidence I've got that she doesn't know about."

"What's going on?" my mum said.

"Please. I have to find her. Can you call her?"

The policeman was looking confused. In the back of my head I could hear Mum remonstrating, a strident tone to her voice. My brother was looking at me as if I were a little mad and my dad had got out of the car and was leaning on the roof.

"Will you help me?"

Just then I saw the silver Mini. It was coming from round the side of the hospital. I waved but it moved slowly ahead, going over the speed humps heading for the exit.

"Wait here," I said.

I rushed off, across the car park. I couldn't run, exactly, but I went quickly, my arm in the air, waving all the time. Florence didn't see me, though. The silver Mini moved on up to the barrier and would in a matter of seconds leave the car park and head out on to the roads. I pushed myself on but was suddenly overtaken by my brother, who shot past me and headed for the car. Just as the barrier went up he got to it and banged on the window.

Florence immediately got out. She looked indignant, holding her shoulders straight. I couldn't hear what Dan was saying, but then I was within calling distance and she turned and saw me walking towards her.

"Ashley," she said.

"Here," I said, hobbling towards her, out of breath, holding up the keys.

"Those are yours," she said, a touch of irritation in her voice. "We found them on the boat. You must have dropped them during the fracas. I removed the GPS."

"No, look! This," I said, fiddling through to get hold of the memory stick.

I was puffed. I had too many words in my mouth to say, too much explanation. I held the memory stick out to her and she looked at me as if I was mad.

"This!" I said. "This is what I want you to have."

"A lipstick?"

"A memory stick. I saved it all on this. The photographs, the recording of the conversation. I put it on my laptop and then I saved it on to this. I didn't tell you earlier because I thought it had gone into the water. I thought there was no point if it was gone. But it didn't fall into the water, it must have come out of my pocket when I was fighting with them. It must have dropped. It's not wet or anything."

She was staring at me, her forehead puckered.

"The *evidence* is here." I took hold of the memory stick and edged it off the main key ring. Then I offered it to Florence. Her face was blank and then the words seemed to settle, to take hold. She gave a sigh. She put her hand out and took the memory stick. I noticed her nails, still yellow, bits of varnish chipped off.

"You mean the photos of Marty Robertson and DI Brennan are on this?"

"And the recording of the conversation."

"They're all on here?" Florence said, turning to Dan and smiling widely.

"Yes, yes, yes!"

"Then we've got Robertson. We've got him! And DI Brennan. We've got the both of them."

206

I looked at Dan. He gave me a reassuring smile. It was his memory stick after all.

Florence was rummaging about in her bag. She pulled out a small plastic wallet. She dropped the memory stick into the bag.

"Ashley, you have to go home now. You leave the rest of this to me."

Dan took my arm and we headed back to my mum and dad standing by their car.

TWENTY-EIGHT

I wrapped the West Ham shirt as well as I could. It made an oblong parcel. The corners were awkward, a mess. I sighed. Some people's gift-wrapping skills were perfect. Stylish paper, sharp edges, a ribbon tie and a beautiful label. I started with good intentions but it always got complicated. The corners seemed geometrically wrong and wouldn't fold at right angles. The paper was too bulky and didn't lie smooth but bunched up. I ended up sticking it down with layers of sticky tape so that it was almost impossible to open.

I looked at the ungainly shape and felt myself getting upset. I swallowed and held my lips tight in a straight line. I would not cry again. I would not. I picked up the label and wrote on it. *To Tyler, hope you are feeling much better. All the best, Ashley Littlewood.* There was probably no need to put my surname but I did anyway.

I placed the Christmas present on top of my bag. Inside there were others: a gift for Beth's mum and dad from my mum and dad; a jigsaw for Sara from me; a vintage blouse for Beth that I'd bought from eBay.

It was Christmas Eve, two weeks since that night on the river.

The bump on my head had gone down and I had recovered from the physical exertions of those few days when I had been on fast forward, running around the streets of Rotherhithe as if I was some kind of junior police officer. PC Littlewood. *Stupid, stupid.*

I saw myself in the mirror. I was wearing the Fair Isle jumper that I'd bought in the charity shop in Wanstead weeks before. I thought it would a raise a smile. On the front of it was a reindeer. It looked daft really but I was only going to Beth's house with Dan. He and Beth had been spending more time together and tonight Beth was looking after Sara while her mum and dad went out for the evening. I didn't intend to stay for long. I knew that Beth and Dan would want to be alone and that they were only asking me because they felt sorry for me.

I was taking Tyler's present so that Beth could pass it on to her aunt and uncle when she saw them on Christmas Day. Tyler was back living with his mum and dad for a while, recovering from his ordeal. The wound on his head had needed to be re-stitched and there was talk of cosmetic surgery in the future. His ankle had been operated on again and he'd been dehydrated and generally knocked about from his time at the building in Bryan Street. He would get better but it would take time.

I hadn't been back to school. I hadn't been able to face the rush and activity of the school day. I had a couple of coursework pieces to give in and I'd managed to do that. The rest of the time I'd spent with Dan or my mum and dad or just soaking up daytime TV.

Marty Robertson and his son had been charged with the murders of Joseph Lindsay and Stuart Lister. Phil and Scot had been charged with conspiracy. They were all in prison waiting trial. The shop at Mile End was closed. DI Brennan was still being interviewed. Florence had come to see me on an official visit to tell me what was going on. I'd expected her to look sober and neat, a suit and some dark shoes, a briefcase or leather shoulder bag. Instead she seemed just as offbeat as when she'd been undercover. She had a scarlet blouse over jeans and boots and on the top was a long woollen overcoat that looked like it had been a man's. Her nails were painted scarlet.

I was pleased to see her like that. I would have been nonplussed if she had looked any different. After she finished telling me what was happening, I asked her about Jimmy Connelly. She shrugged. They'd questioned him, she'd said, but he denied knowing anything about anything. *He will be the fish that slipped away, but I doubt that he'll have many friends round here*, she said. Before she left she told me that her real name was Martha Fitzgerald. She gave me a hug and told me to keep in touch, leaving me her real mobile phone number. I thought of the four mobiles in her bag and wondered which one of them belonged to Martha Fitzgerald. When she left I put the name out of my mind. I wished her happy Christmas. For me she would always be Florence Monk.

I put my bag of gifts by the front door and went into the living room. I flicked through the cards that we had received and thought about this night, a year ago, when I broke up with Tyler.

It was evening. Not a time when I usually visited him. I had paused before opening his garden gate because I wondered if his parents would be there.

They weren't.

Tyler had opened the front door as bold as brass. He was wearing his glasses and the hoodie that he'd had on down Alexandra Avenue except the hood was down. He smiled when he saw me and stood back to hold the door open further so that I could walk in.

"I saw you selling drugs," I said, abruptly.

He opened his mouth to speak but nothing came out. He used a single finger to push his glasses up his nose. It gave him the look of a schoolboy, not a drug dealer.

"You swore you didn't do it. You lied to me."

He didn't answer.

"Don't ring me any more," I said, "I don't want anything to do with you."

I walked off. I crossed his street for what I thought was the last time. I gripped the carrier bag and looked down at the pavement until I got home. I ran up the stairs without anyone seeing me. Once in my bedroom I pulled the wrapping paper off the gift. I tore the paper to bits and let it float on to the floor. I even pulled at the shirt but the fabric was unbreakable and it lay unperturbed on my bed while I cried until my eyes were sore.

So much had changed in twelve months.

"Ashe? You ready?"

I could hear my brother calling me from downstairs.

"Coming," I shouted.

It was the first time I had been out of the house in two weeks. My dad was giving us a lift to Beth's. I got in the car carrying my bag and I felt this sense of déjà vu. I sat in the back and made myself listen to the corny music that my dad was playing. Inside I was barely able to acknowledge the feelings that I had, the emotions that had been churned up by the things that had happened. I had owed Tyler a favour and I had tried to do it for him, almost getting him and myself killed in the process. It had turned out all right, though, and I had retreated back into the corners of my life, but those places seemed very chilly now.

I still had this heat inside me. This feeling that singed my chest and throat whenever I thought of him.

Would it ever cool?

We arrived at Beth's and I got out with my bag of gifts. My dad drove off and we were just about to open the gate when Dan grabbed my arm.

"Sis, I need you to do me a massive favour."

"What?"

"Me and Beth, we thought we'd go out for a couple of hours? Just to the pub. There's a few kids celebrating Christmas there?"

I nodded and then it dawned on me. Dan was asking me to babysit for Sara so that he and my best friend could go out together on Christmas Eve. For a second I felt a kind of muted fury, but it passed. Why shouldn't they go out and enjoy themselves?

212

"You want me to look after Sara?"

"Would you? It wouldn't be for long." He put his arm round me and gave me a hug. "You're so good to me."

I walked behind him up the path and the front door opened without us even knocking. Beth had obviously been watching out of the window, waiting for us. I looked at her and couldn't help but smile. She was wearing the polka-dot leggings with a floaty top that I hadn't seen before. In her hair she had a feather clip that looked old. She saw me looking.

"Got this at Barnardo's in Leytonstone. Two quid!"

"It looks great," I said, going in the hallway.

Her Burberry mac was hanging on the newel and her bag was sitting on the floor. It looked as though she was ready to go. I felt a pang of hurt. There wasn't even going to be time for a quick chat, a beer, a sit-down in the living room before she and Dan shot off to the pub and left me to listen in case Sara woke up.

"Thanks so much for doing this," Beth said, as if Dan had telepathically communicated my willingness to her.

"That's all right," I said, straining to smile.

She walked to the front door, her coat flapping round her.

"It's nine now," Dan said. "We'll be back before eleven."

"What if your mum rings? What shall I say?" I called.

"Mum knows you're babysitting. Don't worry."

The front door closed. I stood very still for a minute feeling depressed. They'd been so sure of me they'd told her mum in advance. How predictable was I? I dropped my bag of presents and listened for a moment to the silence of the house. I sighed. Perhaps there would be something good on the television. I walked to the living room and opened the door.

Then I stood very still, holding my breath.

Tyler was sitting on the sofa. In front of him was a stool and his foot, in fresh plaster now, was resting on it. I stared at him. He didn't look up at me. He had his glasses on and was reading a book. I frowned. It was *1984* by George Orwell.

"What are you doing here?" I said.

"Waiting to see you."

I looked at him with astonishment. His face looked thin and the scar by his eye was still red. He moved a little stiffly on the sofa, as if he was still in pain somewhere. I tried to think of something to say but couldn't and there was an awkward silence.

"Terrible jumper," he said.

I looked down at the reindeer stretched across my chest. "It's vintage."

"It's not, it's odd!"

"I like it."

We'd talked freely the last time we were together. Sitting on a boat in the freezing Thames. Then there was lots to say. Now there was nothing. Eventually I spoke.

"I wanted to say how sorry I was. . ." I started, patting down the reindeer on my jumper.

He shook his head. "No need for that."

"There's every need. I was stupid, stupid. . ."

"Come and sit down," he said, patting the cushion next to him.

I looked at my feet. I didn't know what to do. Part of me was furious. This had been arranged by Beth and Dan and probably Beth's mum and dad knew about it. My shoulders squared up with irritation but when I looked up and caught his eye it faded and I felt myself soften and my face broke into a smile.

He looked back at his book. He turned the corner of the page down and closed it and laid it on the floor.

"Still reading George Orwell?" I said.

"I'm a slow reader. In any case, a few things happened this year and got in the way. Come here and sit next to me."

I walked across the room and sat down and folded my arms.

"You can relax. I'm not going to jump on you," he said, pointing at the cast on his foot. "I couldn't if I wanted to."

He ran his fingers down my arm.

"Thank you for saving my life," he said.

I reached across and took his glasses off. I put them on the floor on top of his book. Then I leaned forward and kissed him.

An award-winning author, Anne Cassidy has written over twenty books for teenagers. She is fascinated by the way ordinary people can be sucked into crime and forced to make agonizing moral decisions.

Praise for Anne Cassidy's books:

"*Totally gripping*" BOOKS FOR KEEPS

"*Dark, chilling and clever . . . Anne Cassidy reminds me of Minette Walters or Ruth Rendell*" Celia Rees

"*Always compelling*" TELEGRAPH

"*Compassionate and unflinching*" GUARDIAN, Jan Mark